Blinded By Love

Nicole Hill

D1367670

<u>*Acknowledgements*</u>

Praises to the Almighty, without him none of this would be possible.

Mama, I told you one day I would make you proud of me. I feel I've succeeded since you mention my book to EVERYBODY you come in contact with.

I want to thank my siblings, especially my brother Patrick. He's always on his job promoting me. ☺

Nichole Martin, my CoCo. Words can't express how thankful I am to have you in my life. We haven't seen each other in over 20 years, but when my first book dropped you supported me and made sure your friends did the same. I just want you to know that what you did, didn't go unnoticed.

Gabrielle, Jaleel, and Jaquille you are my inspirations. I love you guys past the moon and back.

To EVERYBODY that supported my first book, THANK YOU SO VERY MUCH.

To my GEICO family (FPM) you guys rock. Thanks for the support.

[3]

Chapter 1

Christi lay on her bed contemplating whether she wanted to go to the mall. She decided to call her best friend Cymone to see what she was up for this afternoon. When she answered the phone, Cymone sounded a bit dry.

"Hey girl...What are you getting into today?" Christi asked.

"I really want to go to the mall and get those new Jordan's," Cymone replied, looking through her closet for something to wear.

"How about I come pick you up, and we head on over to the mall to get them?" Christi suggested.

"Okay, I'm ready whenever you are... Oh I almost forgot, Tasha here with me, is it okay if she tags along?" Cymone asked.

"Girl, you didn't have to ask me that," Christi said letting out a slight laugh. "I'll be there in 10 minutes," Christi said, hanging up the phone. She grabbed her purse and car keys, making her way to Christi's house.

When the girls arrived at the Macon mall, it was crowded as usual, so they decided to walk around and check out the scenery. Cymone and Christi together always turned heads. Christi's smooth golden brown complexion

with her hypnotizing light brown eyes made the fellas weak in the knees. Her shoulder length jet-black hair was always pinned up. She had one dimple in her right cheek that came out of hiding every time she smiled. Cymone's caramel complexion was flawless except for a few freckles on her nose, which complemented her eyes, a beautiful shade of gray. Her long hair was naturally curly. She was so beautiful people always mistook her for a model. Tasha stood out from both of them with her dark cocoa brown complexion, her exotic dark brown eyes capable of melting the hearts of men around her. She never liked to show her petite and curvy figure, so she mostly wore baggy jeans, t-shirts, and tennis shoes. Christi and Cymone stayed in high heels, tight jeans and fitted shirts, always showing their tight bodies.

When the girls walked inside Footlocker on a mission for Jordan's, the store was packed. They walked around until they found what they were looking for. With perfect timing, the handsome footlocker employee approached them.

"You girls need help with anything?" He smiled.

Tasha held up the Jordan Retro 7's. "Do you have these in a seven?" The young man asked if she wanted them in red and black, or red and white. "I'll take the red and black," Tasha replied with a sweet voice.

"I need a nine in black and red also," Cymone blurted out before he could walk away.

"And I need the same in an eight," Christi interjected. The young man nodded and took the shoe from Tasha, walking towards the back. Once he ducked behind the stock room door Tasha hit Cymone on the arm and started gushing. "Girl he is fine, and he smelled so good…I saw how he was looking at you."

"Yeah I saw that too… Y'all need to stop he works here. He has to be friendly to the customers, so he's just doing his job." Cymone said.

Tasha nodded in fake agreement. "Yeah, you right."

"He was friendly to me and Christi, but he was extra friendly with yo ass," Tasha teased, giggling a little.

Before Cymone could respond, the young man walked back up to them and handed each of them a box. The girls checked their shoes and approved them. They proceeded to the counter to pay for their shoes. Cymone squeezed past the young man and another customer, and he swiftly grabbed her arm. "Wait! Before you go…can I have a word with you?" he asked Cymone quietly. She turned her head and looked at Tasha and Christi, who were watching like it was a movie. They both smiled and walked to the cash register. Turning back to him, Cymone asked, "What you want to talk to me about?" The young man could not help but be caught up in Cymone's beauty introducing himself.

"I'm Maurice… And you are?" he said.

"Cymone…My name is Cymone." She replied with a huge smile on her face, sticking out her hand.

Maurice eagerly reached out and shook it gently. "Nice to meet you… Now, I don't normally do this but it's something about you that got me wanting to get to know you better. I know that's not possible right now since I'm here at work, but can I have your number and maybe call you later when I get off?" Maurice asked.

Cymone thought about it for a minute and decided to give him her number. "Can I see your phone?" She asked him. Maurice reached into his pocket and handed Cymone his phone. She put her number in his phone and handed it back to him.

When Cymone turned to go pay for her shoes, Maurice took her shoes and said, "You good, I'll take care of those for you." He placed the shoes in a bag and handed them to Cymone with a seductive look on his face.

Cymone looked Maurice up and down. She leaned back causing a dip to form in her hip and proudly said, "I can buy my own shoes." The wrinkle in her forehead showed Maurice that she was offended. She didn't need his money, she had her own!

"I know you can... Just let me do this for you?" Maurice asked.

Cymone softened her facial expression. "Thanks."

When she walked out of the store, Tasha and Christi were waiting on her. They both were asking multiple questions at the same time. Cymone could not process what they were saying. She placed her hands over her ears and screamed.

"One at a damn time." She yelled. "Y'all sound like a bunch of damn rats," Cymone scoffed at her friend jokingly.

Christi tapped her foot placing her hands on her hips. "Well, tell us what he wanted?" She said.

"If you nosey chicks must know, he asked for my number and paid for my shoes," Cymone said as she slung her hair to the side and strutted off, leaving Tasha and Christi standing there with their mouths wide opened. They looked at each other and ran to catch up with Cymone.

"Look chic I'm hungry," Tasha said. "Let's go to the food court and grab a bite to eat." She suggested.

"Yeah, Cymone is paying for everything since she got her shoes for free," Christi replied with a giggle.

Cymone laughed and said, "You silly, but I got y'all." Amused by the reaction from her girls, Cymone asked, "What y'all want to eat?"

Tasha chuckled. "We can get anything we want?"

"As T.I. would say, you can have whatever you like!" They all laughed, heading for the food court.

The girls decided on Chinese food from China Max. They ordered their food and found a table.

As the girls were eating, Tasha blurted out, "Ain't that the boy from Footlocker?"

Cymone turned around to see him walking in their direction. "Yeah that's him." She said nonchalantly, hiding her curiousity. He hadn't seen them yet, so she took a moment to really get a look at this man.

"That brother is good looking," Christi chimed in.

"Yes, he is." Cymone agreed smiling.

"Check out the walk, he's bowlegged in one leg." Tasha sighed softly.

When Maurice noticed Cymone and her girls sitting in the food court, he walked over to them and said, "Hey ladies...Do you mind if I join you?"

Tasha pointed at the empty chair, "Have a seat," she offered.

"I didn't mean to interrupt, but I couldn't just walk by and not say anything," Maurice said smoothly, looking in Cymone's direction.

Christi looked at Tasha and mouthed, "Walk to the bathroom with me." When the girls stood up, Christi said, "Mone we'll be back."

As Tasha and Christi walked away, Maurice never looked away from Cymone. "You have cool friends."

"Yeah, they're okay," Cymone replied.

"Cymone, you are a very beautiful girl, but of course, you already know that," Maurice said.

"Thanks. You're not so bad yourself," Cymone giggled.

"Can I ask you a question?"

"Go ahead..." she answered shyly.

"What is it that you're looking for in a man?" Maurice asked bluntly. "That is, if you're looking for one."

"Honesty, trust, respect, and understanding... I want a man that will be man enough to admit his wrong doings." Sitting back in her seat, she continued. "I can respect any man that can come to me and say 'Baby, I messed up'. When you hear things from the street committee nine times out of ten it's not as bad as they make it." Cymone spoke frankly, looking Maurice directly in his face. "I just want to be given the opportunity to decide what I want to do when things go down. I need honesty at all times, not someone who will assume that I'm gonna flip out and leave when shit gets hard." She could feel her attitude creeping into her words..

"Ain't that what most chicks do?" Maurice questioned, leaning in closer to her.

Cymone placed her hand under her chin. "I mean it depends on what the mess up was. If you cheated with a random chick, you met at a club one night and had no intentions of it happening again, I would be hurt, but I can forgive," Cymone responded. "We all make mistakes…but if you're constantly messing with the same chick over and over, then I feel I need to let you go because obviously you want to be with her. You can't make the same mistake more than once," Cymone said now folding her arms across her chest.

Maurice sat back, thinking for a moment. "I can dig that… I believe I can give you everything you just said. And more, if you give me the chance."

Cymone giggled and a smart smirk came across her face. This man was bold. "Oh really? You want me to be your girl just like that, huh."

"I do. When I saw you in Footlocker, there was something about you that got me wanting to know you more." Maurice was unwavering.

Cymone started to blush a little. "Something? Something like what?"

Maurice grinned and took a deep breath. "For one, those eyes are hypnotizing. And you have great taste in shoes…If you give me a chance, I promise you I'll always be that man for you and more."

Cymone started to feel a little rushed and uncomfortable in her seat. Where were her girls? "I don't want to rush into anything, but if you're willing to take things one day at a time, I'm willing to see where it goes." She didn't know how to take this man or what his intentions were for the moment. That would soon change.

6 Months Later

Cymone could not think about nothing, but Maurice. They had been on a few dates, and she was beginning to fall for him. They talked and texted every single day. He would call her every morning, texting her throughout the day just to see where she was and if she needed anything. She could not believe all the happiness she was feeling. She had finally found a man that respected her; he was honest, faithful and dedicated only to her. And to have found him at the mall! She knew this was different. So when Maurice asked Cymone to move into his house with him, she allowed the thought to grow on her. But when she brought it up to her mother, Laila did not approve.

Cymone walked into the kitchen to find her mother sitting at the kitchen table drinking a glass of red Moscato. It was still light out.

"Baby girl, come sit with me so we can talk about this moving thing again." Laila motioned for Cymone to sit in the chair next to her.

"What's there to talk about Ma?" Cymone said folding her arms across her chest in protest. She did not understand what her mother's issue was. He wanted her to move in with him, and she wanted to do it. To Cymone, that was the end of it.

"Cymone, what's the rush to live with Maurice?" Laila asked gently.

"Ma, I love him, and he loves me." Cymone responded to her mother with attitude in her voice.

"Baby girl, that's not a good enough reason to move in with somebody you have only known a few months. How can you say you love him, and he loves you, when the two of you are still getting to know each other?" Laila put down her wine glass and touched her daughters arm. "Don't get me wrong, Maurice seems like a good kid, and from what I see, he seems to care a lot about you. But baby girl hear me when I say the Maurice you're dating now, is not going to be the same Maurice you'll be living with." Her mother spoke bluntly, trying to get her to understand where she was coming from.

"Ma, you worry way too much. This is not something we just decided to do overnight. We've been talking about this for weeks now, and I'm ready Ma. Please don't fight with me on this," Cymone said to her mother as she held her head down.

"I'm not fighting with you. I just want what's best for you," Laila reached out, lifting Cymone's chin. They gazed at one another, eye to eye. "Promise me that you will call me every day just to let me know you're okay?" Her mother asked.

Cymone replied sarcastically. "Every day, ma?"

Laila replied, "Yes, every day… And if you can't or don't want to call, shoot me a text and let me know you good. Can you promise me that?" Laila asked her daughter.

"Yes Ma, I can promise you that." Cymone reluctantly told her mom, with only a few reservations. Her mom was budging.

With hesitation in her voice, Laila let it out. "I guess I'll give you my blessings."

Cymone jumped out of her chair and wrapped her arms around her mother, planting kisses all over her face. "THANK YOU. THANK YOU. THANK YOU." Cymone ran off to her room to call Maurice to tell him the good news.

Laila sat there watching her baby with tears in her eyes. As her wine glass found its way back into her hand, she took a sip and let her eyes and mind wander. Gazing out of her kitchen window, she thought about her only son Jarvis who was killed at just nineteen years old. Jarvis was a good kid who did not get into any trouble. He worked his entire four years of high school and still managed to graduate with honors. He was doing everything he could to be successful. During his first year of college, he would call and text Laila every day just to let her know he was okay. During summer break, Jarvis was supposed to come home for a few days. He texted Laila and told her that he would be leaving out after the party was over and that he should be there no later than 2:00 AM.

Laila had been so excited that she tried her hardest to not fall asleep. She tried staying up to wait for him to get there, but she found herself waking up on the sofa. She immediately looked at the clock; it was three o'clock in the morning and Jarvis was not there yet. She checked her phone, but she had not received a call or text. Laila's motherly instincts kicked in, and she knew right then that something was wrong. Calls to Jarvis' phone repeatedly went to voicemail. A strange feeling in her gut began to bubble. She tried to ignore that gut feeling that something was wrong, but it kept nagging her. Just then, she heard a knock at the door. She dreaded the walk to the door but it had to be made. What if it was him? It seemed like every step she took wore her down. When she finally made it to the door and opened it, two police officers were standing there. At the sight of them, all Laila could do was fall to her knees and scream, "No, not my baby." Cymone heard her mother screaming, so she ran to the living room to see what was wrong. She noticed the officers at the door and her mother on the floor, crying hysterically.

Cymone rushed to her mother and fell to the floor beside her. "What's wrong ma, why are you crying?" She looked up at the officers with angry, confused tears in her eyes. "What did y'all do to my mother?"

The taller officer cleared his throat. "We're looking for Laila Jones."

Her mother looked up and wailed. "I'm Laila."

"Ma'am do you know a Jarvis Jones?" Laila screamed out, already knowing what was coming next.

Cymone stood and addressed the officers with a trembling voice. "That's my brother, did something happen to my brother?"

"Ma'am I hate to have to inform you, but Mr. Jones was killed last night."

It seemed like the world stood still. Cymone could not fully process what the officer said. She could see his mouth moving at this point but could not hear what he was saying. By this time her mother had passed out on the floor.

The shorter officer spoke into his radio. "We need paramedics at 431 Hightower Blvd."

The kitchen phone started to ring, snapping Laila out of her thoughts. She wiped her eyes before answering the phone. "Hello…Yes, hold on." She placed the receiver on the counter and yelled for Cymone. "Cymone…Cymone…Telephone."

"Take a message, I'll call them back," Cymone yelled back.

"Who's calling?" Laila asked.

"Ms. Jones this is Christi," the lady on the phone said sweetly. Christi started to explain to her that she had been trying to reach Cymone, but she never answers her calls. "I called her cell, and she sent me to voicemail. Since she has been serious with Maurice, I hardly see or talk to her. I mean I'm happy she found love and all, but I miss my friend," Christi said with frustration in her voice.

Laila was at a loss for words. She did not know Cymone had cut her friends off. "Christi, I am really sorry to hear that. I was under the impression that the two of you were still hanging out." Her mother stated.

"No Ma'am, I haven't hung out with Cymone in about three months," Christi said.

"Hold on, baby," Laila stated. "Cymone, get your butt in here right now."

Cymone walked into the kitchen looking confused. "What Ma…Why are you yelling?" She asked.

"Why haven't you talked to Christi in three months?"

Cymone popped her lips. "I have talked to her...What's the problem?" Laila held the phone out for Cymone to take. Before grabbing the phone, she asked, "Who is it?"

"It's your friend Christi." Laila replied.

Cymone rolled her eyes and took the phone from her mother. "Hello...I'm good...I've been busy Christi. It's nothing personal. Look I was in the middle of something, I'll call you back." Cymone hung up the phone and handed it back to her mother.

Before Cymone could walk off, Laila decided to make a point. "I guess you don't have time for your friends because Maurice needs all your time? Cymone, you don't let no man come in between your friendship with your girls. Those girls will be there when that man won't. I know I taught you better than that," Laila was disappointed.

"Ma, Maurice doesn't have a problem with my friendship with Christi. I chose to back off from her. I just get tired of all the hating. Every time I would talk to her and say something about what Maurice did for me, she would get mad and start acting funny towards me. So I stopped talking to her. I don't know what she told you, but when I wanted to talk to her she acted funny towards me. Now that I haven't been accepting her calls, all of a sudden she wants to talk. Well Ma, it doesn't work that way. I don't need that drama in my life." Cymone bluntly told her mother.

Laila just looked at her daughter in disbelief. She could not believe Maurice had a hold over her to the point she would sever friendships. "Baby girl, if you're neglecting your friends now, what' is gonna happen when you move in with him?" She walked out of the kitchen, shaking her head at her daughter.

Chapter 2

"Hey baby, how was your day?" Maurice watched as the smoke fell from his lips.

Cymone straddled him, grabbing the blunt out his hand. She hit it three times before speaking. "It was okay, my mom gave me a lecture about moving in with you, and then she gave me the lecture about Christi. She called the house today, and I guess she told my mom I hadn't been talking to her." Cymone said.

"Did you tell your mom why you haven't been talking to Christi?" Maurice asked.

"No, I made up a story about her acting funny towards me because I'm always talking about you." She answered while she blew smoke in his face.

"Baby, you should have just told your mom the truth," Maurice said.

"My mom already doesn't want me to move in with you. If I tell her you fucked Christi, and I'm still with you, but mad at her, I'll never hear the end of it. And she definitely won't let me move. I'm trying to forget the shit. That's why I've been avoiding her. I don't want to hear nothing she has to say," Cymone said, feeling herself starting to get upset.

Maurice coughed, passing the blunt back to Cymone. "Baby, I'm really sorry about that. You know I was drunk that night, and she just took advantage of the situation. I tried to…"

Cymone pressed her fingers to his lips before he could finish. "I don't want to talk about that today, tomorrow or any other day. I chose to forgive you and continue building on what we have. Maybe one day I'll find it in my heart to forgive Christi, it's just not gonna be today. I would have never done no shit like that to her. I would have expected that shit from Tasha but not Christi," she stated.

[21]

Maurice mumbled under his breath. "Shit, she wouldn't even let me hit it."

Cymone looked up at Maurice. "Baby, did you say something?"

Kissing Cymone softly on the lips Maurice smiled. "I didn't say anything baby." Damn, Maurice thought to himself. Did I just say that shit out loud? This weed got me bugging. He had to get it together, and fast.

****

Since Cymone had been a no-show in Christi's life, she and Tasha had become closer friends. They started hanging out and talking on the phone more. Sometimes Tasha invited Christi to her mom's house for Sunday dinner, but she had never made it. Once Tasha told Christi that the menu for this Sunday consisted of homemade mac and cheese, BBQ ribs, cabbage, meatloaf, rice, lima beans, cornbread, and sweet potato pie for dessert, she was all but ready to eat.

When Christi arrived at Tasha's, she was introduced to Tasha's mom, Cyndi, and her little sister, Latrice. They exchanged small talk for a while, then Tasha took Christi to her room until it was time to eat dinner.

Once inside Tasha's room Christi said, "Your mom seems cool, and you have the cutest little sister. I just got one question though?" Christi sat down with a confused look on her face.

"What's that?" Tasha responded.

"Why did your Mom cook all that food just for three people?" Christi asked.

Tasha smiled. "My mom cooks big every Sunday. A few family members and friends usually stop by to get something to eat and there is always plenty of food. I really think they caught on to the Sunday dinners and just decided to make that day the day to visit."

Christi laughed. "I don't blame them, everything smells so good."

"My mom can throw down in the kitchen. You will see for yourself in a little bit. Changing the subject, Tasha was ready to talk for real. "Have you talked to Cymone?"

Christi sighed heavily. "I talked to her briefly the other day. I had to call her house phone because every time I call her cell phone she sends me to voicemail. Since she has been with Maurice, she has really changed. In the beginning, I thought he was the nicest person. I was happy that she was happy, but now...now I just don't know." Christi vented to Tasha.

"Can I trust you with something?" Tasha asked.

"Yes, you can trust me with anything." Christi stated matter-of-factly.

"I knew I could…Well, remember that night we were all at Shon's place?" Tasha said.

Christi nodded in agreement. "Yeah that was the night Cymone got drunk and passed out."

"Exactly." Tasha said. "Well, while you were trying to sober Cymone up, Maurice tried to get with me. First, he was just making small talk but then he started playing with my hair telling me how beautiful I was. I started getting uncomfortable, so I got up to leave, and he grabbed my arm and pulled me back down on the sofa. He began telling me how sexy my lips were, and how much he wanted to kiss them. He started stroking my arm and whispering things in my ear. Then he had the nerve to try to kiss me! When you and Cymone walked up he stood up and kissed Cymone like nothing happened." Tasha went on to explain.

Christi shook her head in disbelief. "That bastard…Did you tell Cymone what he did?" Christi asked.

Tasha sighed heavily. "I tried but she is so gone over his ass, I just didn't say anything."

"Tasha, I feel I can tell you the real reason Cymone isn't talking to me." Christi took a deep breath, switching positions in her chair. "About three months ago we were

[24]

over to Maurice's place playing tonk for shots. Well, I'm not much of a tonk player and neither was Cymone." Christi stated, as she crossed her legs. "We got wasted pretty fast...You know how Cymone is when she get drunk, she passes out. I was in no condition to drive so Maurice told me I could crash on the sofa. He gave me a pillow and a blanket, and he went to bed. I was twisted, the room was spinning, I tried to lie down, but that only made it worse. I could not get comfortable for shit. I tried to lie back down but quickly had to get up. I almost didn't make it to the bathroom." Christi said shaking her head.

Tasha laughed. "That Cuervo had you calling on Earl?"

Christi smiled. "Girl yeah, I was praying to that porcelain God. Once I called on Earl, I felt better. I rinsed my mouth, washed my face with some cold water and went back to the living room and laid down. I was dreaming about T.I. and all of a sudden I started feeling really good. I felt a head between my legs, so I started rubbing his head. At this point, I didn't know if I was asleep or awake. When I opened my eyes there was Maurice with his head between my legs licking away. I tried to push him up off me, but he just climbed on top of me and pinned my arms down. Screaming was out of the question because he was pressing his body weight on me, I could barely breathe." Christi felt the pain of her words as they came out, and she looked up at Tasha, wiping her eyes.

"Even though I was struggling he didn't enter me roughly. The sick bastard acted like he was enjoying himself. He started saying shit like. 'Damn girl, this pussy good,' and 'you feel better than Cymone.'" Christi was still disgusted with it all.

"Wait a minute. He was doing all of this with Cymone in the other room?" Tasha asked.

"Yup... I'm lying there crying, begging him to get off me. When he finally got off me, and was putting on his boxer, Cymone walked in. I'm thinking since we were girls and she sees me crying she would know sleeping with him wasn't what I wanted. Maurice instantly started trying to plead his case. He told her he was drunk, and I took advantage of him." Christi wiped her eyes once more, trying to get it together. "The fact that she believed that lie hurt more than anything. We fought that night Tasha. I didn't want to hit her, but I had to defend myself. I left Maurice house that night a broken woman. I could not believe the events that had just taken place." Christi said sobbing.

"I cannot believe this; you have to let her know." Tasha demanded.

"I've been trying to talk to her. It's even worse now, because Last week I found out I'm pregnant. Tasha, what am I going to do?" Christi stated throwing her hands up in defeat, sobbing.

Tasha grabbed Christi and hugged her tight. "Damn, I can't believe she put you off for him." She said, craddling Christi. "Why didn't she question him about being in the living room with you?" Tasha was in disbelief. "I believe what you just told me, and even if he hadn't of tried me like he did, I would still believe you. I mean she should know you wouldn't do any mess like that with her in the next room." Tasha said shaking her head.

"Tasha, I'm 18. I don't have a job. I can't take care of a baby right now. I don't believe in abortion so, that's not even an option for me." Christi started panicking, running her fingers through her hair.

"Whatever you decide I'm here for you."

"Thanks, that really means a lot. Maybe one day she will sit down with me and hear the whole story, but until then I'm just gonna continue praying."

Chapter 3

Cymone was so happy to be finally living with Maurice. Her first night there, they sat in the living room and watched TV.

"Who were you with before me?" Maurice asked unexpectedly, as they flipped through the channels.

The question caught Cymone off guard. They had been together for a while, and he had never brought this conversation up before. Cymone looked at Maurice puzzled. "Where did that come from?"

Maurice shot Cymone an angry look, raising his voice. "Answer the fucking question," He boomed.

Cymone could not believe her ears. Maurice had never raised his voice or cursed at her. She responded quickly to his question. "I had one boyfriend before you, and his name was Josh."

"Did you do the things you do with me with him?" Maurice continued the interrogation.

Cymone looked at Maurice as if he had lost his damn mind. "Why all of a sudden you want to know about my past relationships?" She huffed.

Maurice jumped up off the sofa and snatched Cymone up. He threw her up against the wall so hard she hit her head and almost passed out. As he grabbed her by her throat she could hear him gritting his teeth. "If I see you so much as look at another dude I'm gonna beat the shit out of you...Do I make myself clear?" Cymone looked up to see a fire in Maurice's eyes that she had never seen before.

Cymone was so scared she did not know what to do. She could not speak, she just nodded her head. Maurice let her go but Cymone didn't move, she just stood there crying. Maurice went back and sat on the sofa as if he hadn't just threatened her. Cymone slowly walked back to the sofa and sat down. What her mother had said to her started playing in her head. 'The Maurice you're dating now is not gonna be the Maurice you're living with.'

Maurice slapped Cymone across the face. "You don't hear me talking to you?"

Cymone was so deep in her thoughts that she did not hear Maurice talking to her. Cymone rubbed her face, the sting of the slap stunned her. "Why you hit me Maurice?"

"Because I'm sitting here talking to you, and you acting like you ain't hear me." Maurice spat. "Where were you just then? Were you thinking about that nigga Josh?" Maurice didn't give Cymone time to respond before he said. "Bitch if you tell me you were, I'm gonna beat your motherfucking ass."

"I wasn't thinking about no damn Josh. I just thought about something my mom told me. I can't believe you. I'm going to bed."

Cymone lay in the bed crying wondering what she had gotten herself into. Maurice had never raised his hand to hit her before; she did not know who the man in the living room was. Cymone wanted to pick up the phone to call Christi but felt she may not want to talk to her after the way she has been ignoring her. She decided to call Tasha instead. When Tasha answered the phone, Cymone was relieved. Just hearing a familiar voice calmed her a little. "Hey Girl, what you doing?"

Tasha was surprised to hear Cymone's voice. She hadn't spoken with Cymone in months. "Wow, what pleasure do I owe for this call?" Tasha said sarcastically.

Cymone laughed. "Girl, I've been hella busy. I realized I hadn't talked to you in a while, so I was just checking in to see how you were doing." Cymone answered nervously.

"I'm good. How you been doing?" Tasha replied.

"I couldn't be better. I'm living with Maurice now, and things are good." Cymone said trying to sound cheerful.

"That's good Cymone…I don't mean to rush, but I was in the middle of doing something. I'll give you a call back later okay." Tasha replied.

With tons of disappointment in her voice, Cymone said. "Okay." When she hung up the phone, all she could do was cry herself to sleep.

****

"Why didn't you talk to her?" Christi asked Tasha.

"I've called her several times, and she sends me to voicemail. She sounded like she had been crying. She said she was living with Maurice now, so they probably had a fight. Things ain't so good at home now she wants to call. That ain't cool with me. I just wanted to show her how that shit feels." Tasha crossed her arms.

"Tasha…"

"What? Don't make time for me when it's convenient for you." Tasha bluntly stated.

"I feel you…I gave up trying to call her, when she's ready to talk to me she'll call." Christi said with a sigh.

[31]

"How about Maurice called me and asked if we could get together again. He acts like we kicking it." Christi said with a disgusted look on her face.

"Dude is a straight up mental case. Does he know you're pregnant?" Tasha asked.

"No, I didn't tell him about the baby. After he asked me that shit I hung up the phone. He's still been calling, but I send him to voicemail."

All Christi could do was shake her head about the situation. It really hurt her to know that Cymone could be that dirty. Just then, Tasha came up with an idea.

"Christi, what you should do is answer his calls and record everything he says." The plan was already forming, the wheels were turning. This could work.

Christi looked confused. "Why you want me to do that?"

"Cymone sounded like she had been crying. So maybe if she hears the shit for herself she may wake up and realize that the guy she so in love with is a dirt bag." Tasha explained.

Christi started feeling Tasha's idea. "You know what Tasha, I never thought about that. The next time he calls me I'm gonna do just that."

"Have you decided what you're gonna do with the baby? It's getting closer and closer to your due date."

Christi rubbed her big belly. "I know. No, but I'll be glad when this part is over. I can't see my feet, and I still have two more months to go." She said with a frown.

"You okay?" Tasha asked.

"Yeah, the baby just kicked me really hard," Christi answered getting up to walk the pain off. Before she could take one step she doubled over in more pain. Tasha jumped up and guided her back to the sofa to sit down. Christi looked up at Tasha with tears in her eyes. "Something isn't right." She yelled out as pain shot through her spine and stomach.

"Sit right here. I'm gonna call the paramedics." Tasha tried to remain calm while looking at the pain in her friends face. Tasha hung up with 911 and instructed Christi to breathe as the nurse had showed her. Christi yelled out in pain, writhing as it took over her body. Tasha did not know what to do. She felt powerless as she rubbed Christi's back, telling her everything was going to be okay. When the paramedics arrived, they laid Christi down on the stretcher, checking her vitals as they her up to the baby monitor. After a few seconds the paramedic got up and got moving. The baby's heart was beating too rapidly.

[33]

"We have to get you to the hospital STAT." The paramedic quickly started to get her ready to go.

Tasha could see the fear in Christi's eyes. She assured her friend that everything was going to be okay. "I will be right behind you. These nice people are going to take real good care of you." She tried her best to assure Christi.

As they were loading Christi in the back of the ambulance, she yelled out to Tasha. "Call my mom for me, please!" Tasha felt her fingers shaking as she dialed Christi's mother's number, but she did not get an answer. Tasha left a message explaining what happened and what hospital they were going to take Christi too. The ride was bittersweet. She knew Christi did not want the baby in the beginning, but as the months had passed by she had begun developing a bond with the baby. Now here was a possibility she might lose the baby that she had just come to terms with.

When Tasha walked through the hospital doors, her phone began ringing. She looked at her caller ID and noticed it was Christi's mom calling back, so she quickly answered. "Hey Ms. Pat, I just made it here…I don't know yet…Yes, we're at Coliseum Medical." She told Christi's mom. Pat wanted to know what happened. Tasha began to explain. "We were sitting down talking and all of a sudden she doubled over in pain. I didn't know what to do so I called the paramedics." Christi's mom told Tasha that she was on her way. "Okay, I will see you when you get here." Tasha hung up her phone and walked over to the nurse's station. She asked where she could find Christi Parker's room. The nurse told her that a doctor would be out shortly to speak with her about Ms. Parker's condition.

A few minutes later Christi's mother walked through the door. She had worry written all over her face. She walked up to Tasha. "Have you heard anything yet?"

Tasha was relieved that her mother was there. "The nurse just told me that the doctor would be out shortly to speak with us about her condition." she responded.

Just as they were about to sit down a short bald head man wearing a white coat approached them. "Are you here with Ms. Parker?"

Pat spoke up. "Yes, I'm her mother, Patricia Parker."

The bald head man shook Pat's hand and introduced himself. "I'm Dr. Jordan...I am sorry to inform you that your daughter has suffered a miscarriage. It's unknown at this time exactly what caused it. It may not have a cause; These things happen without any warning sometimes."

"How is she?" Pat asked with worry and pain in her voice.

"She's resting now. We gave her something for pain. I want to keep her overnight for observation." Dr. Jordan replied.

"Can we go see her?" Pat wiped the tears before they could fall from her eyes. Her daughter needed her, she had to be strong.

"Sure, right this way." Dr. Jordan said.

Tasha and Pat followed Dr. Jordan to Christi's room. When they walked inside, Pat rushed straight to her daughter and hugged her tightly. "I'm so sorry baby." She coddled Christi as she stroked her hair.

Christi smiled weakly and whispered. "It's okay, Ma. My son is resting with the Angels now."

Pat looked at Christi with tears in her eyes. "It was a boy?"

Christi nodded. "Yeah, it was a boy, and he was so beautiful Ma. He had a head full of curly black hair. He looked like a healthy 7lb baby."

With eyes were stretched wide open, Pat said in a shocked tone. "7lbs."

Christi smiled. "Yes, he was 7lbs."

Tasha walked up to the bed and hugged her friend. "I'm so sorry Christi."

Christi was sad but relieved at the same time. "You don't have to be sorry Tash. It's not your fault. Having him wasn't in God's plan for me. When I found out I was pregnant, I didn't want to keep him because of how he was conceived. Regardless how I feel about Maurice, I couldn't abort him because he was also a part of me. I have been tormenting myself for months trying to figure out what to do. I even thought about keeping him. I started to feel a connection with him." Tasha rubbed her friend's shoulder as she purged her soul. "I would talk to him, sing to him, and read to him. I prayed and gave it to God to handle. I just didn't know it would turn out like this." Christi spoke as she held back tears.

Tasha and Pat could see the hurt on Christi's face, but she was trying to be strong. Christi was acting as if it was no big deal when they both knew that was not the case.

"Christi, you don't have to sit here and front with us like you ain't in pain." Pat said. Baby, don't hold those emotions inside, let that shit out." Pat hugged her daughter. "Like you said he was a part of you, so grieve for your son in your own way."

Out of nowhere Christi broke down, yelling and screaming. Pat did not say a word. She just held her baby in her arms. Tasha could not take it, so she stepped out of the room. When she stepped into the hallway, her cell phone began vibrating. It was Cymone calling. She wiped her face and got her emotions together. "Hey girl." she said.

Cymone heard the sorrow in Tasha's voice. "Is everything okay Tasha?" She asked.

"Yeah, why you ask that?" Tasha responded.

"It sounds like you've been crying," Cymone probed Tasha.

"It's that obvious?" Tasha replied sniffling.

Cymone was starting to get concerned she wanted to know what was going on. "Yes, are you okay?"

"I'm at the hospital with Christi."

Cymone gasped. "Is she okay…What happened to her?"

Tasha wanted to tell Cymone what was going on, but she knew it was not her place. "Cymone, I'd rather she tell you," Tasha said. "I'm sorry, but you haven't been there for her lately, and I just don't feel comfortable sharing her personal business with you. If she wants you to know, she will be the one to tell you, not me. I hope you understand where I'm coming from," Tasha bluntly stated.

"I totally understand." Cymone felt the sting of Tasha words. Had it really come to this? "I haven't been there for her...I've been avoiding her for a while now," Cymone admitted to herself.

"I think you should come visit her," Tasha suggested.

With hesitation in her voice Cymone responded, "I'll think about it...Will you just tell her I asked about her?"

I will, just think about what I said. The two of you have been friends way too long to act this way." Tasha disconnected the call and went back inside Christi's room. She noticed Christi was resting, and Pat was sitting in the chair beside her bed reading a book.

When Pat looked up, Tasha said, "I see she's resting, so I'm gonna go. When she get up tell her I'll be back later on to check on her."

Pat smiled. "I sure will. Thanks for being there for her."

Tasha gathered her things from the room. "No need to thank me Ms. Pat, Christi is my girl. I love her like I love my own sister." Tasha insisted. "Do you need me to bring you anything back?" She offered.

"No baby, I'm good," Pat replied. Tasha left, and Pat continued reading her book, as Christi slept her pain away.

Chapter 4

Cymone sat on the sofa contemplating whether she wanted to call Christi or not. She had not talked to her in so long she was beginning to really miss her. She didn't know why it was so easy for her to forgive Maurice and not Christi. Just then Maurice walked in the house and by the look on his face he wasn't in a good mood. "Hey Baby, what's wrong?" She asked.

"Look, don't start all that hey baby shit. I ain't in the mood for it." Maurice spat. Maurice went to the kitchen and looked in the refrigerator to get a beer, but noticed there weren't any more left. He slammed the refrigerator door and stormed in the living room furiously. "What nigga you done had in my house?"

Cymone looked confused. "What you talking about? Nobody has been here." She protested.

"Look bitch, I had three beers left in the damn refrigerator, and now there's none in there. Yo dumb ass don't drink beer. Who the fuck you had in my house?" Maurice demanded angrily.

Cymone knew what was about to happen next. Regardless what she said, from that point on he was not going to believe her. He had drunk so much yesterday that he forgot he drunk those beers himself before he went to bed. "Maurice, I didn't drink your beer and nobody has been here."

Maurice walked towards Cymone and slapped her so hard, her head snapped back. He had hit her before, but never with that much force. The blow temporarily dazed Cymone, and once she came to she covered her cheek with her hand and glared at Maurice with all the hate she should muster in her eyes, but that only infuriated him more. "Oh bitch, you look like you wanna do something. You wanna hit me? I dare you too." He taunted Cymone as she got up, grabbed her keys, and headed for the door. Maurice grabbed her by the hair before she could make it to the door. "Where the fuck you think you going?" Maurice said slyly, yanking her back so hard that Cymone could feel her hair being ripped from her scalp.

"Let me go Maurice. I'm going to my mom's house." Cymone yelled as she struggled to get free. "I can't do this anymore. All you do now is hit me and call me out my name. I don't even know who you are anymore. "Cymone cried.

Maurice didn't say anything. He just punched Cymone in the face knocking her out cold. He paced back and forth talking to himself. He didn't know who the fuck

Cymone thought she was, but leaving him was not an option for her.

After several minutes of being out cold, Cymone started coming to. When she opened her eyes, all she saw was Maurice standing over her. She didn't know if he was gonna hit her again or what so she just laid there. Maurice held his hand out to her to help her up. Cymone hesitated before grabbing his hand. Cymone stood in front of Maurice scared to move. Maurice looked at Cymone's face with so much compassion in his eyes. "Baby, I'm sorry. I didn't mean to do it, you just make me so mad sometimes." Maurice apologized with sweet sincerity in his voice. "The thought of you being with another man makes me crazy. I'm sorry Mone." He pleaded, still holding her hand. "I promise I will never put my hands on you again." Maurice said with tears in his eyes.

Cymone's head was telling her to leave, but her heart told her to give him another chance.

"Please don't leave me Mone! I promise I'll never put my hands on you again!" He begged her, trying to change her mind.

Cymone gave Maurice a skeptical look and said through her own tears. "Maurice I can't take this no more." She took her hand back, pressing it against her chest. "All you do is hit me and accuse me of doing things I'm not doing. You had drunk those beers last night before you went to bed. If you don't believe me, go look in the bedroom. The beer cans are still in the bedroom on the dresser." Sobbing, Cymone continued. "In the beginning you were so sweet to me. You made me feel like I was the only girl in your life." She wiped the tears from her eyes. "Now you treat me like the shit on the bottom of your shoes. I don't go out anywhere Maurice. I have neglected my friends for so long they don't want to have anything to do with me now. I promised my Mom I would call or text her every day just to let her know I'm okay. I text her, but I haven't talked to her because I know as soon as I speak to her she's going to know something is wrong." She cried profusely at her reality. "I don't want to hear the 'I told you so' from her."

Maurice leaned his forehead against Cymone's forehead and whispered. "I'm gonna do better baby I promise. Give me another chance to prove to you I can be the man you fell in love with again." Maurice started kissing Cymone's tears away. He held her so passionately. Her heart started breaking. She knew she should leave but right at that moment, she felt the old Maurice. She just didn't want to let go of what she was feeling.

Maurice laid Cymone down on the sofa and made love to her like never before. When they were finished, Maurice ran a tub of hot water for Cymone. He placed lavender scented candles around the tub. He even remembered to add the bubbles she liked. While Cymone was in the tub soaking her pain away, Maurice was in the kitchen cooking her something to eat. He was determined to make things up to her. When he heard Cymone come out of the bathroom, he fixed their plates and placed them on the table. He lit some candles and turned Pandora on to the R&B station. He had definitely set the mood. If this didn't say sorry, he didn't know what else to do.

Cymone walked into the kitchen. Her hands flew to her mouth at the sight before her, she gasped. She looked at Maurice with tears in her eyes and he mouthed. "I'm sorry." He walked over to her and pulled her chair out for her. Once Cymone was seated in her chair, Maurice took his seat across from her.

Cymone looked down at her plate and smiled. "Everything looks so good." She complimented.

"I did this all for you." He chuckled hoping all was forgiven. Maurice had prepared T-Bone steaks, grilled shrimps with a garlic butter sauce and baked potatoes.

Cymone cut a piece of her steak and took a bite. She moaned in pure delight. The steak was so juicy, tender, and seasoned just right.

Maurice smiled. "It's good huh?" He boasted.

Cymone took another bite of her steak and nodded in agreement. "It's very good." She said. "Who taught you how to cook?" Cymone asked.

Maurice jumped up. "Damn, I almost forgot." He went to the refrigerator, pulled the bottle of wine his manager had given to his employees out and poured them each a flute full.

"Damn baby, you going all out." Cymone stated.

Maurice didn't want to keep telling her how sorry he was, so he decided to show her. "Mone, I'm for real I will never put my hands on you again. I sit here and look in your face, feeling pain, knowing I'm the reason your face is swollen and bruised." He took a moment get the words right. "I will spend every day making this up to you," Maurice said.

Cymone picked her flute up. "Let's toast to new beginnings." She suggested.

[46]

They tapped their flutes together, sipping the wine as they finished eating their dinner. Cymone was in heaven. Maurice had never gone out of his way to prove he was sorry before. That night, while lying beside Maurice, she prayed that he would always treat her this way.

Chapter 5

After Maurice's cousin had contacted him, he went straight to Christi's house to ask if that was his baby she lost. Tasha picked Christi up from the hospital for Ms. Pat, who had to work. When they arrived at Christi's house, Maurice was waiting in the driveway.

Christi looked up frowning at him. "What the fuck?" She spat. It was a shock to see him, especially today, especially in her driveway. A shiver shot through her body, chilling her to her core.

"You want me to keep going?" Tasha asked.

Christi really was not sure what Maurice was doing at her house, but he wasn't about to scare her. "No. I live here! He's not running me away from my own home." Christi sounded confident stepping out the car.

Maurice immediately approached her. "Can we talk?" He had an unreadable look on his face.

Slightly irritated by the nerve of him, Christi brushed him off. "We have nothing to talk about," as she walked off.

Tasha followed tooting her nose up in disgust at Maurice. When the girls were safely in the house, Tasha said, "The nerve of him…What is dude's problem?"

Christi was curious as to why he was at her house. "I don't know, but he needs to get his shit together." Christi replied.

"Christi, I think you need to call Cymone and let her know what's been going on." Tasha suggested lightly, knowing it was a sensitive moment.

"Why bother? She made it perfectly clear where she stands." Christi said nonchalantly.

"She called me yesterday, and I told her I was in the hospital with you. She wanted to know what was wrong, but I told her you would have to be the one to tell her. I suggested she call you but she just said to tell you she asked about you." Tasha explained hurriedly, trying to change her friend's mind.

"Cymone ain't gonna call me. It's been too long. Do you know this is the longest we've ever gone without talking to each other since we became friends?" Christi was sad, and she missed her bestfriend. "I'll call her one day and see if she answers my call, but not today. I tried so hard to contact her to talk to her about that night, but she refused to take my calls." Christi stared off into space. "I love her

[49]

like a sister Tash, but if she's gonna fall out with me over a nigga that clearly is not committed to her then so be it.

"I understand…I wonder what that psycho wanted with you."

"He probably found out about the baby. One of the nurses that took care of me is related to him. She knows me and Cymone use to hang out, so she probably called him and told him I was there." Christi informed Tasha.

"If she did that you can have her fired, that's a HIPPA violation. You are not supposed to give out any personal information!" Tasha felt frustrated. This whole situation just kept on getting messier and messier.

Christi sighed heavily. "It's over and done with. My son is gone. All I have of that night are the memories and in due time those too will fade away." She wiped away her tears. "I appreciate you for being here with me. You have really been a good friend to me. Who would have thought that you and I would be better friends than me and Cymone," Christi scoffed.

"Yeah, it's funny how things changed," Tasha laughed.

****

When Maurice left Christi's house, he went over to his homeboy Nick's house. He needed to talk to somebody about what his cousin had told him. After he told Nick what happened all Nick could do was shake his head.

"How the hell you sleep with your girl's best friend and get her pregnant?" Nick asked Maurice.

"So you telling me you wouldn't sleep with Christi?"

Nick shook his head. "That's not what I'm saying." He stated. "Christi is a very attractive woman, and any man would be happy to sleep with her. But why did you, of all people, sleep with that girl, knowing she is your girl's best friend? As if that was not bad enough, you sleep with her while your girl was in the next room. Dude, that's some foul shit." Nick scolded. He was confused about why Maurice felt that Christi would even talk to him after all that has happened.

"Man, I don't care about all that. I just want to know if that was my baby. All that other shit you talking is irrelevant." Maurice insisted.

"That's your problem man. You don't care about nothing but yourself. You came over here for advice, right? Well, I'm advising you to leave well enough alone. Christi lost the baby. If it was yours, it's irrelevant now. What is knowing gonna do?" Nick argued. "You act like Christi is gonna just up and want to be with you or something. Is that it?" Nick questioned. "Are you secretly in love with that girl?" He probed.

"Ain't nobody in love with that girl, but if she was carrying my baby, I had the right to know." Maurice protested.

"Maurice, are you listening to yourself? From what you told me about that night, you practically raped the girl." Nick spat. "Man, do you really think if the baby lived she was gonna keep it?" He tried to talk some sense into Maurice, but it didn't seem to be working. "Man, you have a beautiful girl at home, leave well enough alone."

Maurice jumped up in anger and stormed out of the house. Nick shook his head at his friend, leaning back on the sofa to finish watching TV.

****

Cymone sat in the living room, flicking through the channels for what seemed like forever. When she finally got up, Maurice had already left, so she relished in the quietness. The night before had been heaven, and the scene replayed in her mind over and over. He had cooked and showered her with so much love, but she knew that it would not last long. Cymone wanted to go visit with her mother. She gently stroked her cheeks and quickly remembered she would have to wait until the swelling and bruises were gone. What was going on between her and Maurice would stay between them. She wished she could talk to somebody about it, but she did not want people judging her for staying with him. She longed to talk to Christi, but she knew that her former best friend would probably would never speak to her again. Still she wanted to know why she was in the hospital. After battling with herself over the thought, Cymone picked up the phone and dialed Christi's number. Close or not, she cared about Christi's wellbeing. As the phone rang quietly in her ear, her nervousness returned and forced her to just disconnect the call. Just when she was about to call back, her phone rang. It was Christi calling her back. Cymone answered the call on the second ring. "Hey, Christi."

"Hey, yourself...When I saw your number on my caller ID, I thought I was seeing things, it's been so long," Christi was nervous too.

Cymone giggled. "Yeah, it has been a while. I want to apologize for that. I knew you wanted to talk to me about what happened, and I refused to hear your side of the story." She admitted.

"Cymone, you don't know how you made me feel. I love you like a sister and for you to turn your back on me for a nigga really cut me deep." Christi explained. "There I

[53]

was standing there with tears in my eyes because your boyfriend literally raped me, and you wanted to fight me." Christi said getting emotional.

"Rape, girl Maurice didn't rape you...Why would you say that about him?" Cymone insisted. Here she was, back with this shit.

"You think I had sex with him willingly?" Christi questioned with a sarcastic chuckle. "Mone, that boy got you so blinded by love you don't even believe your own eyes. Did you ask yourself why he was even in the living room with me when the two of you had been in bed for hours?" Christi demanded an answer trying to hold back her tears. "How did I take advantage of him? Mone, we have been friends too long for you to let him come between us. I would have never done that to you. If you were put in the situation I was in, I would have believed you over my man any day because I know you wouldn't hurt me like that." Christi wiped her tears.

Cymone wanted to believe what Christi was saying, but she could not go against Maurice. It just didn't feel right. "Why would Maurice lie about you taking advantage of him?" Cymone shouted.

"Why would I lie about him raping me Cymone?" Christi spat. "Did Maurice tell you that he came to my house the other day or that he calls my phone repeatedly asking me if we can get together again?" Christi yelled. Christi was getting frustrated with Cymone. She could not believe that she was so blind to Maurice that she could not see the truth. "Tasha told me you called her, and she told you I was in the hospital. She also told me she wouldn't tell you why. Cymone, I had been calling you for months trying to tell you what was going on, but you wouldn't talk to me. I was pregnant Mone, by Maurice." Christi blurted out angrily.

"Here you are trying to manipulate me, lying on my man saying he raped you. You know damn well that didn't happen and if you was pregnant it sure as hell wasn't by Maurice. I get it now, you just don't want me to be happy." Cymone screamed.

Christi shook her head in disgust. She was not believing what she was hearing. "Girl, you are being manipulated, but it ain't me doing it. I know everybody wants to be in love at least once in his or her life, but damn Mone you stupidly in love. I never thought I would see the day when you let a man run over you. I've said what I had to say, you don't have to believe me, the damage is already done." Christi spoke. She realized it was easier for Cymone to believe him. That way she could keep living her little

[55]

fairytale life. But this was her best friend! "That dude is no good. If he would do that to me while you were in the next room. I can only imagine what he does when he is not around you." Christi said somberly. She really felt sorry for Cymone. "Are you that desperate for a man that you would put up with his lies and cheating? I mean for God sake he raped your best friend and got her pregnant." Christi spat wiping the stream of tears that fell down her face.

Tasha took the phone from Christi. "I hope you will be woman enough to apologize to her when the truth comes out." Tasha spat and hung up the phone, hugging her friend. She knew that she was hurt. "When the truth comes out, she'll come back." Tasha whispered as she consoled a hysterical Christi.

"Tasha, that shit hurt so bad. I mean why...Why won't she open her eyes and see the truth?" Christi cried. Tasha felt that deep down, Cymone knew it was the truth. She just doesn't want to believe it. "Just give her time, she'll eventually come around.

Chapter 6

Maurice walked in the house and noticed Cymone sitting on the sofa fuming. He looked at her with a frown in his face. "What's your problem?"

She stood up and got directly in his face. She looked at him for a minute then asked. "Did you get Christi pregnant?"

Maurice flashed a cocky smile. "Is that why you sitting here with steam coming out your ears, you think I got your friend pregnant." He smirked. "Mone, come on now...I told you she took advantage of me while I was drunk. Where is all of this coming from?" Maurice questioned.

"Why were you in the living room with her when you had been in bed with me?" Cymone asked.

Maurice walked off. "I don't know who you think you are questioning me like this. I told you what happened that night, and that's it." Maurice barked, becoming angry.

Cymone started asking more questions back to back. "Why did you go to her house the other day and have you been calling her to hook up?" She asked.

"Damn. What the fuck is this...Ask Maurice a million and one questions day?" He spat.

Cymone folded her arms across her chest. "Well did you?" Cymone demanded an answer.

"I'm only gonna say this once and after today I don't want to hear shit else about it. No…" He roared. "I haven't been to her house. No, I haven't been calling her, and if she's pregnant it's not by me." Maurice insisted. "Are you satisfied now?" He asked.

Cymone picked up her phone and dialed Christi's number. When Christi picked up, Cymone said, "What day did he come to your house?"

Christi responded, surprised. "He came by here earlier, like earlier today. I was just getting home from the hospital."

Cymone knew in her soul that Christi was telling the truth, but she wanted proof. "What does he have on?"

"He has on some blue jeans. I don't know what kind. A red polo shirt, some red and black Jordan's and a fitted hat."

Cymone stood there listening to her best friend tell her exactly what her boyfriend had on. Cymone did not say thank you or goodbye, she just hung up the phone. She would talk with Christi later. Tears ran down her face like a faucet, "How can you stand there in my face and lie to me Maurice? Christi just described everything you got on.

How would she know what you got on? Answer me." She demanded.

"Look Cymone, I don't know why you sitting there believing that girl. I told you I ain't been over there." He protested against the allegations.

"Maybe what she said about you raping her is true too. I'm out of here Maurice. I can't stand to be in the same room as you." She cried. Cymone headed to the door, and Maurice grabbed her, telling her she was not going anywhere. Cymone snatched her arm away from him and without thinking slapped him in his face. As the sting of the slap ran through her hand, it was quickly followed by a pang of fear. Maurice rubbed his cheek and glared at her with those menacing eyes. Cymone knew right then she had fucked up.

She was acting off pure emotions and immediately regretted hitting him. Not because she didn't mean it, but because of what he might do next in return. Maurice didn't say anything. He drew his hand back as far as he could and slapped her back across her face. The impact alone made Cymone fall to the floor. She just laid there as unwanted tears ran down her bruised cheeks. Maurice stood over her glaring through slitted eyes. "If you ever put your hands on me again, I'll kill you." He spoke calmly. Maurice grabbed his keys and headed out the door slamming it behind him.

Cymone didn't move until she heard his car pull off. She grabbed her phone and texted her mom. "Please come get me."

Ten minutes later Laila pulled into the driveway not knowing what to expect. She just knew her baby needed her. She made sure she had her "little friend" in her purse loaded, cocked, and ready to shoot. After all this time, she still didn't trust Maurice with her baby. Call it a mother's intuition but she knew something wasn't right with him.

Cymone had her bags by the door when her mom got there. She was still crying and looking a hot mess. Laila just looked at her daughter, seething and silent. She didn't need to ask what happened, it was written all over her daughter's face. Laila grabbed Cymone's cheeks in her hand, and turning her head side to side, thoroughly examining the damage done. Cymone kept her eyes down, waiting for the "I told you so" to come raging from her mother's lips, but to her surprise it never came.

Laila took a breath, brushing her hair back, letting it fall into her face again, processing. "Is this all your stuff?"

Cymone nodded. Laila grabbed some of the bags and headed to the car without saying anything else. It was clearly visible how angry Laila was, but there was no need to shout. She figured enough shouting had already occurred in her absence from Cymone's life. Cymone had made the decision to move in with Maurice, even after she voiced how she felt about it. She just hoped that her daughter had learned her lesson, because if Maurice ever put his hands on her daughter again, she was going to have to introduce him to her friend.

The ride home was silent. Whitney Houston's song "I will Always Love You" came on the radio. Cymone turned it up and thought quietly to herself as she mouthed the words. I will always love you, but I can never be with you again.

When they arrived home, Cymone went straight to her old room. Laila did not pressure her to talk. She gave her space, to get all of her emotions out. First thing in the morning, they would have a heart to heart. As Cymone laid in her old bed, gazing up at the ceiling, she couldn't help but think about the night she caught Christi and Maurice together. Could Christi have been telling the truth this whole time? "I feel like such a fool, he's been playing me the entire time." Cymone thought out loud, waiting for some unseen confirmation in her stupidity that never came. She wanted to call Christi to apologize but decided against it. Christi was upset when they talked earlier, as she every right to be.

Laila stuck her head in Cymone's door and asked if she wanted anything to eat. Cymone didn't look up she just replied, "No, I'm okay."

"Get some rest and we'll talk in the morning." Laila said goodnight and left Cymone's room, closing the door behind her.

Cymone turned the TV on and began flipping through the channels. She noticed there was a Murder She Wrote marathon on the Hallmark channel and quickly decided to watch Jessica Fletcher get her detective skills on until she fell asleep.

Cymone's ringing cell phone jarred her out of her sleep. She looked at the clock, and it read 4:15 a.m. She said to herself. "Who is calling my phone this time of night?" She looked at her caller ID and saw it was Maurice calling, she did not know whether she wanted to answer or send him to voicemail. The phone stopped ringing. She sighed softly and rolled back over. Before she could get comfortable, her phone began ringing again. This time she answered on the second ring. "What do you want Maurice?"

"I want you to come home… Why aren't you here Cymone?" He spoke sweetly, as if he really meant what he said.

Cymone rolled her eyes and ran her fingers through her hair. "I can't deal with you and your lies. I'm so tired of you hitting on me Maurice. I can't continue living like this." She vented to him, wiping the tears springing from her eyes. "How can you keep telling me you love me when you keep hurting me?" Cymone stated.

"Cymone I'm sorry about what I did, I really am." Maurice pleaded with her. "I was so angry with you for questioning me about what Christi said. I love you, Mone. I know I fucked up, and I'm really trying to change that. I don't want to be without you," Maurice begged.

"You promised me you would never hit me again, but look what did tonight."

"Mone, please come back home." Maurice said through fake sniffles.

Cymone kept her silence, partially enjoying this moment. "I know damn well Mr. Macho Man isn't shedding tears over little ol' me," she thought, as she listened to him grovel.

Maurice sniffled again. "Baby, please come home."

[63]

Cymone could not believe that Maurice was on the phone begging her to come back home. The hurt in his voice really tugged at her heart. "Maurice, I'll just come back in the morning. My mom wants to talk to me, so after we have our talk, I'll get her to bring me back." Cymone stated.

"NO. I want you to come home now. Your mom is gonna try to convince you to leave me. I'll come get you now." Maurice shouted. "Baby, please let me come get you."

Cymone sighed. "Come on and get me Maurice, but I promise you if you put your hands on me again I'm gone."

Maurice smiled. "You don't ever have to worry about that again. I'm on my way."

Cymone disconnected the phone, quietly got up and got her things together. She knew her mom would be mad when she found out she had gone back to Maurice. Cymone grabbed her bags and walked out the door to wait on Maurice. She hated disappointing her Mom, but she loved Maurice, and she wanted to believe that he would do better.

When they arrived at the house, he got out and walked around to open Cymone's door. He reached for her hand and helped her out the car. He ran and unlocked the door for her. When Cymone reached for her bags, Maurice said, "I'll grab those for you come on in the house."

Cymone simply said, "Thank you."

Maurice replied. "I'm trying to be that and more for you." He kissed Cymone on the forehead and ran back to the car to retrieve her bags.

The next morning Laila awoke and went straight to Cymone's room. Noticing Cymone was gone Laila instantly became furious. She just knew Cymone had not gone back to Maurice after what he did. She picked up her phone and dialed Cymone's number. It rang until it went to voicemail. Laila didn't want to leave a message. She wanted to talk to her daughter. She hung up and called right back. This time a sleepy Cymone answered, "Hello."

"Are you back at Maurice's house?"

Cymone didn't answer.

"Girl, I know you heard me." Laila hissed in the phone. "Are you back at Maurice's house?" She asked again.

Cymone hesitated. "Yes ma, I'm with Maurice."

Laila didn't raise her voice when she spoke her next words. "You texted me yesterday to come get you because he put his hands on you. The next time he puts his hands on you, trust and believe there will be a next time, do not call or text me to come get you. You've made your bed hard now you gone have to lie in it."

Before Cymone could respond, her mother had already hung up the phone. Laila leaned up against her kitchen counter, fuming. She knew it was too early in the morning to drink, but she needed a glass of wine. She reached in the cabinet for her favorite wine glass. It was the one her son bought her for Mother's Day.

She grabbed her bottle of Red Moscato out of the refrigerator, sat at the table and poured her a glass. She was so mad she didn't bother to sip; she drank it without stopping. She could not believe Cymone, but there was nothing she could do. She simply asked God to watch over her baby girl.

Chapter 7

Cymone had been back with Maurice for a few months. Everything was good between them. He hadn't hit her nor had he been staying out late. Maurice had definitely been the perfect boyfriend. Things were going so good between them Cymone hadn't called her mom or Christi. Laila had called a few times, but Cymone didn't answer. She knew her mom was disappointed in her for going back to Maurice, so to keep from feeling even worse about how she left she just didn't answer her calls. Cymone had become an expert at avoiding the situation. She didn't know what to say to her Mom. She didn't know how she would treat her now, and she almost didn't want to find out. Christi, on the other hand, hadn't called at all, and Cymone was okay with that.

When Maurice walked through the door, he kissed Cymone on the forehead and told her to get dressed, he was taking her out. Cymone was dressed and ready to go in less than thirty minutes. She wore her skinny indigo-ridge wash Levis with a black sleeveless turtleneck and her black wedges.

Maurice took one look at her and whistled his approval. "You look good, babe."

Mone smiled. "You don't look bad yourself."

Maurice took Cymone to the movies to see "The Blind Side", the movie about Michael Oher from the Baltimore Ravens. He knew Cymone wanted to see it, so he decided to surprise her. After the movie was over, they walked out and somebody yelled Cymone's name. Cymone and Maurice both turned around to see who had called her name. Cymone looked through the crowd of people looking for a familiar face. Just when she was about to turn and walk away she noticed Josh walking up to them, she instantly panicked. She had not seen Josh in years and here he was calling her name while she was with her boyfriend. Her very abusive boyfriend. Her crazy, might kill Josh and her both boyfriend. Cymone smiled nervously. What could go wrong? "Hey, Josh, how you been?"

Josh smiled. "I've been good how about you?"

Maurice stood there looking from Cymone to Josh. He cleared his throat.

"Josh this is my boyfriend Maurice, Maurice this is an old friend Josh." Cymone introduced the two men. Josh held his hand out to shake Maurice's hand, but Maurice didn't reach out to return the favor. He just looked at it. Cymone knew the good time she was having was over as soon as they got home. Josh stared at Maurice for a few

[68]

seconds before turning his attention back to Cymone. Before he could speak, a beautiful dark skinned girl walked up behind him. She wrapped her arms around his waist. The beautiful girl looked at Cymone and Maurice with a puzzled look on her face.

"Heidi this is Cymone. The girl I was telling you about and her boyfriend, Maurice. Cymone, Maurice, this is my girlfriend, Heidi."

Cymone smiled. "Nice to meet you."

Maurice just stood there looking like he smelled something bad.

"I haven't seen you in a long time, and when I saw you walking out, I wanted to speak to you." Josh then turned to Maurice. "I meant no disrespect to you." Before Josh and Heidi walked off Josh said to Mone. "Take care of yourself."

"You do the same, and it was nice meeting you Heidi." Cymone replied.

****

Maurice started yelling as soon as they walked in the house. Cymone already knew how the night was gonna end. When Maurice was upset, there was no reasoning with him. It was his idea to go to the movies, but there he was blaming Cymone saying she planned to meet Josh there.

Cymone tried to explain to him that she had not seen or talked to Josh in years, and it was just a coincidence he was at the movies.

"Why would I plan to meet him there when he was there with his girlfriend?" Cymone cried.

Maurice slapped Cymone. "Bitch stop fucking lying to me."

Cymone grabbed her cheek and gave Maurice a dirty look. "You promised you wouldn't hit me again. I told you if you ever put your hands on me again I would leave." Cymone grabbed her purse and headed towards the door, but Maurice grabbed her arm.

"Where you think you going?" He barked.

Cymone snatched her arm away. "Away from you." This was all too familiar a scene at this point in their relationship.

Maurice snapped. He grabbed Cymone by her throat. "You honestly think I'm gonna let you leave here to go be with that nigga? I will kill you first bitch." He threatened. Cymone struggled to get loose. "If I can't have you no other nigga will." Maurice spat. She continued to struggle to get free, but that only pissed him off more. He began squeezing her neck. Cymone clawed at his hands trying to get free. She felt the air fighting to get in her

[70]

lungs, and as the pressure built up she knew she had to act..
She stomped his foot as hard as she could. When he let her
go, she ran for the door as fast as she could. Struggling get
the door open, she froze as she heard him running towards
her. Before she could turn around and defend herself, he
was right behind her.

Maurice grabbed Cymone, throwing her to the
ground. She thought it might be over until she felt his boot
kick her, over and over. He began stomping on her, all
over, in a fit of rage. All Cymone could do was scream and
try to protect her face. He kept saying, "You gone learn, not
to lie to me!" Cymone was in so much pain she could not
even focus enough of a thought to let out another scream.
She laid there and begged God to take her life. Maurice did
not stop stomping Cymone until he noticed she was not
moving or screaming anymore. He bent down and shook
her while calling her name, but she did not move. Maurice
panicked. He didn't know what to do. He thought she was
dead. If she was dead how was he going to explain that to
the police?

Maurice called 911 and told the operator that he
found his girlfriend unresponsive and bleeding on the floor.
He gave the 911 operator the information she needed. The
operator assured him that help was on the way. A few

minutes later Maurice heard sirens. He took a deep breath and got into his concerned boyfriend mode. He opened the door and waved them in. He was so hysterical you would think he found her lying on the floor in a pool of blood for real. The way he was carrying on no one would ever suspect he was the cause of her injuries.

One of the paramedics leaned down and checked Cymone's pulse. "She has a pulse, but it's weak." They put the oxygen mask on her face and started an IV. They loaded her on the stretcher and asked Maurice if he wanted to ride in the ambulance with her.

He shook his head and said. "I'll follow."

The tall male paramedic asked. "Is she allergic to anything that you know of?"

"Not that I know of." Maurice replied realizing he didn't know anything about her medical information. They loaded Cymone in the back of the ambulance and sped off as the sirens blasted.

When they arrived at the Medical Center, the paramedics relayed all the visible injuries, and when the doctor looked her over, he yelled. "Get this patient prepped for surgery STAT." They rushed Cymone into surgery.

When Maurice arrived at the Medical Center, a white, heavyset officer approached him. "Are you here for Ms. Jones?"

Maurice nodded. "I'm her boyfriend, Maurice."

"Can you answer a few questions for me?"

"Yes, anything officer."

"Let's start with you telling me what happened to her."

"When I got home I saw her lying on the floor. She was not moving, and all I saw was blood. I called 911, and here we are." Maurice stated with no real emotions.

"Do you know if your girlfriend has any enemies that would want to do her harm?"

Maurice shook his head. "No. She doesn't have any enemies. She hardly has any friends. She and her friends had a misunderstanding a few months back, and they stopped speaking to each other."

"Do you think they could have done this to her?"

Maurice thought for a minute. "No, they aren't capable of nothing like that."

"Do you think somebody broke into your home and she surprised them? Are you missing any valuable items from your home?"

"The door was locked when I got home. I had to use my key to enter. I do not know if anything is missing. I didn't check the house. I came in, found her, and called 911. Now I am here. Is that all you need?" Maurice asked the officer. "I need to go check and see how she's doing."

"Yes sir, here's my card. If you think of anything else, please give us a call." The officer watched Maurice, reaching out to hand him his information.

Maurice took the card, looked at it and put it in his back pocket. He walked up to the nurse's desk and asked the status of Cymone Jones. The nurse checked her computer.

"Ms. Jones is in surgery." She answered. "A doctor will be out to speak with you."

Just then, Laila walked through the doors frantically looking around. She noticed Maurice and walked up to him. "What did you do to my baby?" She yelled.

Maurice put his hands up. "I ain't done nothing to your baby."

The nurse walked over to them. "Ma'am, I'm gonna have to ask you to calm down."

Laila turned to the nurse. "What's going on with my baby?"

[74]

The nurse pulled Laila to the side and told her that Cymone was in surgery and as soon as she hears something, she would let her know.

When the nurse spoke, Laila recognized her voice and calmed down. "You're the nurse that called me?"

The nurse smiled. "Yes, ma'am. When I pulled up your daughter's information, she had you listed as an emergency contact.

"Be honest with me, are things bad?"

"Ma'am your daughter was beaten pretty badly. All I know is they rushed her into emergency surgery."

Laila's knees buckled, and she almost fell. The nurse grabbed her arm and helped her to a seat in the waiting area.

"Ma'am have a seat right here. I'll bring you some water."

With tears in her eyes Laila responded, "I'm fine thank you."

"As soon as I hear something I will let you know." The nurse stated sympathetically.

Laila nodded. "Thank you." Laila gave Maurice a look that could kill. Laila knew in her heart that he had something to do with what happened to her daughter, and she was not going to rest until she found out the truth.

Chapter 8

Christi and Tasha were talking on the phone when all of a sudden Christi got an uneasy feeling. She could not explain what she was feeling, but something was not right. "Tasha let me call you back in a few minutes. I just got this urge to call Cymone." She said. "I haven't thought about her in months and all of a sudden she's heavy on my mind. I'm gonna call her right quick to see if everything okay with her and I'll call you back." Christi dialed Cymone's number. It rang then went to voicemail. Christi hung up and tried again. This time somebody answered, but it wasn't Cymone. When Christi recognized the voice, she started to hang up but changed her mind. "Can I speak to Cymone?" She asked.

Maurice laughed. "I'm sorry, but Cymone is temporarily unavailable right now."

"Look, Maurice, stop playing and put Cymone on the phone. I need to make sure nothing has happened to her.

Maurice snickered. "Funny you say that, something did happen to her. Something bad. I'm at the emergency room now waiting for her to get out of surgery." He laughed.

"Surgery! What happened to her? What hospital she at?" Christi felt her heart beating faster and faster. She had known something wasn't right. "Will she be okay?"

"She at the Medical Center and I don't know what happened to her."

Before Maurice could say anything else, Christi had hung up the phone. Christi called Tasha back. "We have to go to the hospital something happened to Cymone."

"I'm on my way." Tasha responded.

Christi and Tasha walked through the doors noticing Laila sitting in a chair asleep They walked up to her calling her name softly so they wouldn't scare her. Laila slowly opened her bloodshot eyes to see Tasha and Christi standing in front of her.

Laila smiled. "Hey."

With tears in her eyes Christi asked. "What happened to Cymone?"

Laila motioned for the girls to sit down beside her. She grabbed and held both of their hands. "I don't know what happened. Maurice said he came home and found her unresponsive and bleeding on the floor." Laila stated.

Christi gasped. "Oh my God… I felt like something was wrong.

Laila patted her hand. "Don't cry, baby. She's in God's hands now. I've been sitting here for hours waiting for somebody to tell me what's going on."

Before Christi could respond, they heard a doctor say, "Ms. Jones?"

Laila jumped up. "That's me."

The doctor smiled. "Can you come with me?" Laila walked behind the doctor through the double doors.

Once they were behind the double doors, he said. "Ms. Jones, I'm Dr. Hassan. Your daughter has suffered a horrific beating." Laila covered her mouth to muffle the scream that was about to escape her lips. Dr. Hassan placed his hand on her shoulder. "Don't worry she's a fighter. She's stable, but still in critical condition. She has suffered several broken ribs, a punctured lung, and a ruptured spleen. She has some head trauma and a broken hip. We were able to stop the internal bleeding." He explained.

Laila cried out, "Oh my God. Who would do this to my baby?"

"Now, we won't know anything until she wakes up. We placed her in a medically-induced coma to help her with the pain. We will keep her like this for a few days so her body can begin the healing process."

Laila wiped her eyes with the back of her hands. "Can I go in to see her?" She sadly asked.

"Yes, you can go in and sit with her."

"Dr. Hassan two of her friends are also here to see here. Will it be okay for them to come in too?" Laila pleaded.

"Yes, that's fine, but just the three of you. I do not want her to get too worked up. Even though she is in a coma, she can still hear her surroundings." The doctor led them to her room, giving them a moment alone.

Laila, Christi, and Tasha stood around Cymone's bed and held hands. Tasha closed her eyes and prayed for Cymone. After some time of prayers and tears, Christi got up.

"Ms. Laila we're going to go, but we'll be back tomorrow to check on her," Christi said.

Laila looked at Christi. "Why did the two of you stop speaking? You were like two peas in a pod. Tell me what happened?"

"Maurice happened." Tasha interjected.

Christi gave Tasha a look, letting her know now is not the time for that. Tasha got the hint and quickly hushed.

Laila looked at Christi. "What about Maurice?"

"Ms. Jones, it's a long story, and it's not important. Right now, you have enough to worry about with Cymone being here. When she is well enough to go home, we all can sit down and talk about it, but for now your focus should be on your daughter and not this foolishness surrounding Maurice."

Laila hugged the girls and thanked them for coming. Tasha and Christi both promised to return the next day to check on Cymone.

****

When the girls arrived back at Christi's house, Ms. Pat seemed worried. "Where have you been? I've been calling your phone, and it kept going to voicemail."

Christi sat down on the sofa, exhausted. It had been a crazy day. "Ma I'm sorry, but my phone died hours ago, and I forgot to grab my charger before we left," Christi explained. "We just left the hospital with Cymone. Somebody almost beat her to death."

Pat placed her hand over her heart, gasping in disbelief. "Oh my God. Is she okay?"

"Ma, she's messed up pretty bad."

Pat sat down beside Christi. "I can't imagine what Laila must be going through. Do they know who did it?"

Tasha turned up her mouth. "Ms. Laila seems to think Maurice had something to do with it."

"Was he at the hospital?" Pat asked with a suspicious look on her face.

"He was there, but he didn't seem too concerned with what was going on and when the doctor came out to talk to Ms. Laila, he didn't try to see how she was," Tasha tried her best not to let tears fall from her face again.

"Mm-hmm," Christi co-signed, sinking further down into the sofa. "Ma, even when Ms. Laila came back out to the waiting room to get us, he didn't try to follow. I have not talked to Mone in months, but she was heavy on my mind tonight. Something said to call her, I knew it, I knew it!" Christi took a minute to collect herself. "When I called her phone Maurice answered, and I asked him to put her on the phone, but he laughed and said something happened to her, and then he told me she was in surgery." Christi explained. "Ma, in my heart I believe he did it."

"That young man seemed like a good kid." Ms. Pat said shaking her head.

Christi turned her nose up. "Ma, it's all an act. He's the reason Cymone and I haven't been speaking."

"I was wondering why she hadn't been over lately. You two have always been two peas in a pod." Pat stated.

"Ma, I'm gonna tell you what happened between us, but you have to promise not to overreact. I know how you can get so promise me you'll stay calm."

"Chris, just tell me, and after I hear what you have to say, I'll promise you then," Pat said giving her daughter a look.

"No ma, you have to promise me before I tell you," Christi demanded.

"Okay, Christi Janae Parker spit it out. I promise I will not overreact. Is that better?" Pat asked.

Christi proceeded to tell her mom everything that happened the night she was assaulted over Maurice's house.

Pat opened her mouth to speak, "Wh..."

She was interrupted quickly by Christi, "Just listen, ma," she begged. Pat closed her mouth and leaned back on the sofa with her arms folded across her chest. Christi knew she was mad because she had started tapping her foot on the floor. "Ma before I finish telling you, you have to calm down," Christi said. Pat stopped tapping her foot, but she kept her arms folded across her chest. Christi continued telling her mom what took place that night. Pat was ready to kill Maurice by the end of her story.

"You mean to tell me that son of a bitch raped you, then lied to Cymone." Pat yelled. "Baby girl, why didn't you come to me when it happened? I would have taken you to the police to press charges against that sick son of a bitch." Pat questioned Christi. After hearing the story, Pat was convinced that Maurice was capable of hurting Cymone. "I just pray Cymone will wake up before it's too late." Pat said.

****

For weeks, Christi and Tasha went to the hospital to see Cymone. They sat beside her bed talking with her like she was able to respond to the conversation.

"Mone remember when you were dating Josh? He had come over to see you, and I was supposed to be the watch out girl. I ended up getting on the phone with Rick and forgot all about you," Christi said letting out a giggle. "When Ms. Laila walked through the door, I almost shitted on myself. I was so scared and nervous. I was straight stuttering. I sounded just like that man in Harlem Nights. Ms. Laila took one look at my face, then burst through your bedroom door." Christi laughed so hard she got a cramp.

"Did Ms. Laila catch Josh in her room?" Tasha asked laughing.

"Before her mom burst through her door Josh had went out the window." Christi said grabbing Cymone's hand. "Do you remember that?" Christi whispered with tears streaming down her face. Just then, Christi felt Cymone squeeze her hand. Even though her friend was in a coma and not able to speak, at that moment she had let her know she was there with them, and could hear everything they were saying.

Tasha noticed the tears in Christi's eyes. "What's wrong?"

Christi smiled. "She squeezed my hand when I asked her if she remembered."

Tasha held Cymone's other hand. "Okay missy, you have laid up in this bed long enough. It's time to wake up so we can turn up." Tasha demanded. Tasha felt Cymone squeeze her hand this time. The girls sat with Cymone a little while longer, reminiscing over the past. When Ms. Laila walked in the room, they told her about how Cymone had squeezed their hands when they were talking to her. Tears of joy filled Laila's face.

Laila raised her hands up. "Thank you Jesus. Please bring me back my baby." She walked over to her baby and kissed her on the forehead. "Come on back to us baby girl. We all right here waiting for you." Laila pleaded.

Christi hugged Laila and told her they were going to leave so she can have some alone time with Cymone. Christi motioned for Laila to walk out the room so Cymone could not hear what she was about to say. "Ms. Laila, we have been up here every day to see Cymone, not once have I seen Maurice. Don't you think that is strange? I mean if that's his girl, why isn't he by her side through this?" Christi asked.

Laila shook her head in disgust. "I tried to tell my daughter about him, but she wouldn't listen. I put her in the Lord's hand and prayed she would open her eyes." She said. "I don't need her to tell me he did this to her because I know he did." Laila shook her finger in the air. "I'm going to let God handle him. I know he will handle him much better than I ever could. I thank you girls so much for being here with her. I know y'all have not been the best of friends lately, and I'm guessing it's because of the company she has chosen to keep." She said hugging Christi.

"Ms. Laila you don't have to thank us for that. Cymone is my friend regardless of what has happened between us. I still love her." Christi responded.

"What happened between you two? And please, I need to know. It has been breaking my heart and I know deep down it was hurting her too." Laila looked back towards Cymone.

Tasha hugged Laila and let Christi know that she would be waiting in the car. They were going to need this moment alone.

Christi motioned for Laila to have a seat beside her. "Ms. Laila, to make a long story short, Maurice raped me, I got pregnant, and had a late-term miscarriage."

Laila looked at Christi in shock. "What?" She yelled louder than normal. That just wasn't what she had expected Christi to say, especially not now.

The nurses turned to see what was going on, and Laila instantly lowered her voice. "He did what to you? Did Cymone know?" Her mother questioned.

"Yeah I told her, but she didn't believe me." Christi answered.

Laila began biting her lower lip. "I can't believe this shit." She turned to Christi. "I'm so sorry that happened to you." Christi placed her hand on Laila's. "No need for apologies. It's over and done with now. I have moved on from it. I prayed about it and left it with God," Christi bid Laila farewell as she walked towards the doors, back to the car. She hoped God could fix this mess Maurice had caused for them all. She prayed Cymone would make it to know the truth.

Chapter 9

Three Weeks Later

Cymone woke up out of her coma seemingly out of nowhere, and the police were notified to the hospital to question her about what happened the night of her incident. While she waited for them to come, Cymone gazed out the window and thought hard. Maurice had promised her he would never hit her again but there she was laid up in the hospital because of him. Cymone felt she was to blame for what happened because she never should have put her hands on him. Cymone loved Maurice so much that when the police came, she looked the officer in his face and told him she had no clue who beat her. She knew the officers did not believe her, but without her cooperation there was nothing they could do to Maurice. She knew everybody suspected him anyway, but she would never confirm it. That was her man. She knew he would do better.

Another four weeks passed, and soon Cymone was well enough to go home. As they packed up and headed out, she noticed that her Mom was not taking her to Maurice's, but to her house. She knew this was going to be a fight. "Ma, I'm going home not to your house."

Laila gave Cymone a sideway stare. "That low down dirty bastard didn't visit you not one time while you were laid up in the hospital nor did he call to check on you. Do you honestly think I'm taking you to his house?" Her mother spat angrily. "I will not leave you to fend for yourself. For God sake Cymone, you can hardly walk. When you're able to take care of yourself, you can go back over there but until then you're coming home with me." Laila said matter-of-factly.

Cymone poked her mouth out and rolled her eyes. She didn't say anything else because she knew there were no wins with her mother at this time. She decided she would stay there long enough to get her strength then she was going back to Maurice's.

When they arrived home, Laila helped Cymone in the house. "You want to lie on the sofa or do you want to get in the bed?" Laila asked.

"I want to get in my bed if that's okay." Cymone requested.

"That's fine sweetie. You want something to eat too?"

"No, I just want to sleep right now." Cymone replied.

Laila made sure that Cymone was comfortable. "I have a few errands to run. If you need me, just call my cell. I shouldn't be longer than an hour." Laila told her.

"Ma, I'll be fine. Go handle your business." She told her mother.

Laila kissed her daughter on the forehead and walked out of her room. When Cymone heard the front door close, she picked up the cordless phone and called Maurice. The call went straight to voicemail. She hung up and tried it again. This time he picked up. Cymone smiled when she heard his voice. "Hey, baby."

"Where you at?" He asked.

"I'm at my mom's house."

"You don't live with your mother you live with me. Why didn't you bring yo ass home?"

Cymone's voice trembled. "My mom brought me here until I get my strength back."

Maurice roared. "I don't wanna hear all that. Bring your ass home now."

Cymone sighed. "Maurice, my mom is not bringing me there until I can take care of myself. Why didn't you come see me while I was in the hospital?" She asked.

Maurice never answered. He nonchalantly asked. "Did the police come question you?"

"Yeah, they came and asked me a bunch of questions,"

Feeling skeptical Maurice asked. "What did you tell them?"

"I told them I didn't remember what happened."

Maurice was relieved. "Good girl. You know I'm sorry about that. I didn't mean to go there with you. I promise you I'm never gonna put my hands on you again."

Cymone asked him again. "Why didn't you come see me while I was in the hospital?" Cymone could not understand why it was so hard for him to answer that simple question.

"I was so scared when you were lying on the floor not moving." Maurice said truthfully.

With no real emotion, Cymone said. "If you were so scared why you didn't come and check on me? Tasha, Christi, and Ms. Pat came to see me every day."

Before Cymone could say anything else, Maurice interrupted her. "Look, I'm with my boys right now. I'll call and check on you later."

"Oh…okay." Cymone was hurt and disappointed by his words, and it was evident in her voice.

Maurice picked up on her disappointment. "How about I come by and visit with you later? I'll bring you something to eat." He was trying to cheer Cymone up.

Cymone smiled. "You really gonna come see me?"

"Yes baby, I've missed you." Maurice responded, rolling his eyes.

Cymone could not hold in her excitement. "Okay, I love you." She told him.

Maurice hesitated then replied. "I love you too."

Cymone was feeling happier than ever when she disconnected the call. She laid in her queen sized bed and prayed that things would get better. She knew she could never tell anybody what Maurice had been doing to her. Yes, Maurice hit her from time to time and this last time almost took her life but he was sorry, and she knew deep down inside that he really loved her. Why else would he still be with her she thought. He picked up the phone for her and was even going to come by. He must still love her. Cymone drifted off to sleep with thoughts of seeing Maurice.

Cymone jumped up out of her sleep and noticed it was dark outside. She looked at the clock beside her bed, and it read 2:30 a.m. She could not believe she had slept the entire day away. She checked her phone and noticed

Maurice had not called her. Cymone reached for her walking stick and slowly got out of bed. She walked to her mom's room and found Laila was in bed fast asleep. Cymone went into the kitchen to get something to drink and decided to fix a sandwich. While she was fixing her sandwich, she dialed Maurice number. The call went to voicemail, so she hung up and dialed him again. This time the call was answered, but the voice she heard on the other end was not Maurice's.

"Hello?" A sleepy, irritated voice answered.

Cymone looked at her phone to make sure she dialed the right number. When she noticed she had, she thought to herself "Who is this answering my man's phone?" Cymone cleared her throat. Not another woman on his phone, not today. "Who is this?" Cymone demanded.

"Who are you looking for at this hour of the night?" The female voice hissed.

"Why are you answering Maurice's phone at this hour of the night?" She questioned.

"Because he's doing what I was doing before you so rudely interrupted. Look, Maurice is asleep, so I suggest you call him back at a more reasonable hour, I say around 11:00a m. We should be up by then." The female on the other line stated.

Cymone gripped the phone so tight she thought it would break in her hand. "Look, I don't know who you are, but I would really appreciate it if you would put my man on the phone." Cymone spoke through clinched teeth.

The female chuckled sarcastically. "*Your* man?"

Cymone heard a click and looked at the phone in disbelief. "No, this bitch didn't just hang up on me." She dialed Maurice's number back, but this time he answered the phone. "Maurice, who just answered your phone?" Cymone questioned slamming her fist on the counter.

Maurice was slightly irritated. "What are you talking about? This is the first time my phone rang." He said sleepily.

Cymone was now furious; her entire body began to tremble. "Look, don't do that. I just called your phone and some bitch answered." She yelled.

"Look Mone it's late, don't call here with that foolish shit."

Cymone didn't even respond to what he said. She just hung up the phone. She grabbed her mom keys and limped to her car. She was going over there to see who answered his phone because she was not crazy. She knew she dialed the right number, and she knew what she heard.

She just got done lying to the police for this man, and he was playing her for a fool.

When she arrived, there was a car parked in the driveway. Luckily, she had the spare key to the house that she kept at her Mom house. She opened the door and walked inside her old place. It felt strange, almost like she didn't belong here anymore. Once she was inside, she noticed the bedroom light was on. Before she could open the door, she heard the same female voice speaking. "Do you think she's gonna come over here?"

Maurice responded. "Hell nawl, she ain't gone come over here. She just got out the hospital and plus she know better."

Cymone pushed the door open so hard the door handle put a hole in the wall. "Oh, I know better, huh. I thought you were so fucking sleepy." Cymone yelled. "You tried to make me think I dialed the wrong number."

"Mone what the fuck you doing here?" Maurice said, jumping up from the bed.

"Don't I live here? I mean that's what you said earlier when I talked to you. The question is why is this bitch here? In our house? In my bed?" Cymone said pointing her walking stick at the girl in the bed.

Maurice walked towards Cymone with nothing but destruction in his eyes. Usually when Cymone seen that look in his eyes she would back down, but at that moment for some reason, she felt no fear.

Maurice stood directly in her face and said in a whisper. "Why did you bring yo ass over here?"

Cymone looked Maurice dead in his eyes. "What you gone do now, beat me?" She asked maintaining eye contact. "If it makes you feel like a man go ahead, but I refuse to let you keep playing me. I damn near lost my life because of you, but did I leave you? No." She told him getting emotional. "Did I admit to the police you did this shit to me?" Cymone said holding up her walking stick. "No, I was loyal and faithful to you despite the beatings, but no more Maurice. I'll come back tomorrow for my things." Cymone said walking past Maurice over to the bed. The girl lying in the bed looked at Maurice with fear in her eyes. She didn't know what Cymone was about to do to her. If only she knew who the real one to fear was.

Cymone raised her hands. "You don't have to be scared. I'm not gonna do anything to you. I just wanted to look you in your face."

With a smile that could light up the darkest skies Cymone simply said. "Thank you."

Cymone turned to Maurice, shook her head in disgust and walked out. She felt so used but promised herself she wasn't going to shed another tear over him.

Chapter 10

When Cymone arrived back at her mom's house, Laila was sitting on the sofa waiting for her. Cymone walked through the door trying to be as quiet as she could. Laila turned the lamp on and Cymone damn near jumped out of her skin. She placed her hand over her heart. "You scared me. What you doing sitting here in the dark?"

Laila crossed her arms over her chest. "Why are you sneaking in the house?" She questioned with raised eyebrows.

"Ma, I…" Cymone tried to speak, but Laila held up her hand letting her know she didn't want to hear what she was about to say.

"I'm not gonna ask you why you went over there or what happened when you got there. I just hope whatever happened opened your eyes to the truth." Laila firmly stated. "You are a beautiful, smart, intelligent and loving young woman. You're too young to be going through this bullshit with Maurice." Laila patted the seat next to her, gesturing for Cymone to sit down. "He doesn't deserve you, and I'm not just saying this because you're my child." Laila looked deeply into Cymone eyes. "Mone you can have any man you want, why waste your time on somebody who means you no good?"

"Ma, I love him. It wasn't always bad between us," an emotional Cymone said. "I don't know what happened. When I moved in with him, he changed. He became more possessive and abusive towards me. I could never do anything right in his eyes." Cymone cried.

Laila searched her daughter's beautiful gray eyes. "Is he the one that beat you?"

"Yes, Ma he's the one that beat me." Cymone turned to her mother. "He didn't hit me this time." Cymone lowered her head, ashamed to tell her mother how Maurice stomped her like a dog. Cymone twirled her fingers and rocked back and forth. Laila put her hand on top of Cymone's. "It's gonna be okay just tell me what happened."

Cymone stopped rocking and looked into her mother eyes. "He stomped me mommy, he stomped me like I was a roach on the floor. The pain was too much for me. I begged God to take me right then and there." Cymone said breaking down.

Laila wrapped her daughter in her arms and held her tight.

"I was lying there thinking to myself, 'How could this man do this to me and say he love me?' I have seen other people in abusive relationships and I use to always say, why won't they just leave, but I now know that it's not easy to leave." Cymone said wiping the tears from her eyes. "Every time he beat me he would say he was sorry, or he would do something nice for me. He always promised he would never hit me again. I wanted to believe him so badly that I just decided he meant it, over an over."

"Mone, why didn't you come to me?" Laila asked with tears in her eyes.

"Because I knew you would give me the "I told you so" speech and I didn't want to hear it. I had made my bed hard, and I had no choice but to lie in it." Cymone cried to her mother.

"Mone, we all makes mistakes. We all have thought our parents didn't know what they were talking about at some point." Laila spoke softly, touching the side of Cymone's cheek. "I knew Maurice wasn't the one for you, but until you learned that for yourself you would have just thought I didn't want you happy. Christi and Tasha both were at the hospital every day to see you. Even Pat came to the hospital to see you. Maurice did not stop by or call to see how you were doing, not once." Cymone averted her gaze, knowing how wrong Maurice had been to her.

Laila changed the topic, remembering what she really wanted to know. "Cymone, Christi told me what happened. I could not believe for the life of me why you would not believe her. She has been your friend for years. I know she would not do that to you. You have a lot of making up to do with Christi, and you owe her that." Laila scolded. "She was by your side talking with you, praying for you, all the while still dealing with the loss of her baby. Are you gonna press charges against him?" Laila took a breath, waiting for a response.

"Ma, to be honest, I just want to put that behind me. Maurice will eventually get what he deserves. I just thank God I still have my life. I'll let Maurice self-destruct on his own," Cymone just wanted to let it go.

"Mone what happened when you went to his house?"

With so much pain in her voice Cymone said, "He had another girl in the bed we shared. He could not come see me because he was playing house with some other chick. I thought I would want to beat her down, but all I did was thank her. He's her headache now, not mine." Cymone declared.

Laila hugged her daughter and assured her things were gonna get better.

****

Six months past, and Cymone was still trying to get her life back. She and Josh ran into each other again, but this time they exchanged numbers and decided they would try their relationship again. Things seemed to be looking up for her, and Josh was just the man she needed. He began mending the heart that Maurice had broken. After being back together for a few months, Josh brought up the fact that he wanted Cymone to move in with him. Although she thought the idea was sweet, she declined. She told him she would rather them live in separate households because she really didn't want a repeat of living with Maurice. In all honesty, she was afraid, and cautious. She refused to make the same mistake again. Cymone had not heard one word from Maurice since being back together with Josh. The last time he called her, he was locked up for beating on his girlfriend. He had wanted her to bail him out or call his mom to come see him.

Cymone had no intentions of bailing him out, so she called his mother and told her where he was. From that moment she felt truly free. He was behind bars, he couldn't hurt her or anyone again. Cymone still loved Maurice, but she knew she could never be with him again.

Chapter 11

Josh picked Cymone up for a night of fun. He planned to take her to Red Lobster for dinner and then a movie. When Josh pulled into Red Lobster's parking lot, he noticed the same car that had been behind him since he picked up Cymone pull in behind them. He thought it was strange, but he quickly pushed it out of his mind. He got out the car and walked around to open the door for Cymone. As she stepped out of the car, a deep voice taunted her. "Bitch I told you if I couldn't have you nobody else would."

The sound of his voice made Cymone freeze for a moment. "Maurice what are you doing?" she said, looking petrified as she turned to face him.

Maurice stood there with a gun pointed directly at Cymone's face.

Josh was in shock, yet anger shot through his voice. "Put the gun down and its whatever dude."

Maurice laughed, the same maniacal, shiver inducing laugh he used while beating the shit out of Cymone. He was enjoying this too. "You talk a lot of shit. If I were you I would shut the fuck up before this gun goes off accidently," Maurice said threatening to shoot Cymone, inching the gun closer to her head.

"Maurice why are you doing this? We haven't been together in months. I've moved on with my life, and I thought you had too. Leave us alone" Cymone tried her best to keep her composure, trying not to let her fear sneak through her shaky tone.

Cymone closed her eyes and took a deep breath. After letting it out for some strange reason she felt no fear. She looked Maurice in his eyes. "Why you standing here pointing a gun at me? What, you ran out of women to beat?" She spat in his face angrily. Who did he think he was, ruining their night, after almost ruining her life?

"Bitch you need to stop while you're ahead." Maurice shouted.

"What's wrong Maurice, did I strike a nerve?" Cymone taunted him, unafraid of the barrel staring her down. Josh was getting hysterical, trying to reason with the both of them, begging for her life.

Maurice cocked the gun and was just about to shoot. Luckily for Josh and Cymone, a police car pulled into the parking lot before Maurice could let off a shot. The officer saw what was happening and pulled his weapon, rushing out of his vehicle. "Don't do anything stupid, put the gun down!" The officer barked at Maurice. The look Cymone saw in Maurice eyes told the story of how he wanted the night to end. She knew he had every intention of ending her life that night.

Maurice knew there was no getting away with it, so he laid the gun down on the ground and raised his hands in the air never breaking eye contact with Cymone. He said in a whisper to her, "I'll be out soon, this shit ain't over."

Cymone could not move or speak. She just stood there in shock. She couldn't believe she had just talked to Maurice that way and was still breathing. Josh ran over to Maurice and punched him in his face before the cops handcuffed him. "Nigga you are one sick individual. Come near Cymone again and dropping the soap ain't gone be the only thing you gone have to worry about."

Maurice smirked at Josh. "Nigga, you really don't want these problems... Trust me."

The officer read Maurice his rights, handcuffed him and put him in the backseat of his car. Josh wrapped his arms around Cymone. Just the feel of him snapped her out of the trance of fearlessness she was in.

Cymone felt the tears rushing to her eyes. "He was gone kill me."

Josh wiped her tears away. "Baby, you never have to worry about him hurting you." Josh assured her.

The officer walked up to Josh and Cymone. "What happened here tonight?" Josh spoke up for Cymone. He explained to the officer that she and Maurice had dated for a little while but had not been in contact with each other since the breakup. He told the officer that tonight he noticed a car was following them, but thought he was just paranoid. He then told the officer that when he walked around to open the door for her, her ex came from out of nowhere and put a gun to her face.

"Luckily I pulled up just in time before things had gotten real ugly. Well, he's going to jail. I will need you two to come to the station to give a formal statement."

Josh looked at Cymone then turned to the officer and asked, "Can I bring her in the morning?"

The officer nodded in approval and headed to his police car. Before getting into the car, he turned his attention back to Cymone and Josh. "Make sure you come in the morning." Josh took Cymone home and made sure she got inside safely.

When Laila saw the look on her daughter's face, she glared at Josh. "What did you do to my daughter?"

[108]

Cymone spoke up. "Ma, he didn't do anything to me. We didn't even get a chance to enjoy our evening. Maurice showed up at Red Lobster and pulled a gun out on us. If that police officer hadn't shown up when he did, I would not be standing here right now," Cymone explained the situation.

Laila's eyes bucked. "What?"

"Evidently he was waiting outside when we left. I noticed a car behind us but thought nothing of it. When I opened the door for Cymone he came out of nowhere with a gun," Josh added.

Laila could not believe what she was hearing. Where was her glass of wine?

"Ma, if you could have seen the look in his eyes; he really wanted me dead." Cymone began crying hysterically. Laila wrapped her arms around her daughter and held her close to her.

"I'm gonna go. I'll be back in the morning to take you to the police station," Josh said.

Cymone pulled away from her mom and grabbed Josh's arm. "Don't leave." Cymone was really shook. "Ma, will it be okay for Josh to stay here with us tonight?"

"I don't mind if he stays here tonight, but he's not sleeping in the bed with you."

Josh smiled. "I wouldn't disrespect you like that Ms. Laila, the sofa will be fine."

Laila patted Josh shoulder. "I'm going to bed. Mone make sure you get Josh a blanket and a pillow."

Mone went to the hallway closet and got a blanket and a pillow for Josh. After she had made the sofa up for him, they lay together for a little while.

"Mone what did you do to him to make him act so crazy?" He asked.

"Josh, I didn't do anything to him, I don't know who he is anymore. I do know he is definitely not the same person I met," she said holding back her tears. "When I moved in with him he changed. You remember that night you saw us at the movies. When we got home he damn near stomped me to death because he thought we planned to meet." She told Josh. "What happened that made you and Heidi break up," Cymone asked.

Josh sighed. "After that night she started asking more questions about you. She wanted to know why we broke up, had I seen you before that night and did I miss you. It just became too much. She started trying to compare our relationship to the one you and I had. She was real insecure. No matter what I said she didn't believe me."

Josh explained. "She woke up one morning and told me no matter how hard she tried she couldn't be you."

Cymone looked puzzled. "Why was she trying to be me?"

"I guess she thought that was the only way I would want her."

Mone asked curiously. "What did you tell her about our relationship?"

"The only thing I ever told her about us was that we always had fun together. I told her you were not only my girlfriend, but you were also my best friend. If saying that made her feel like she had to become you then I guess I'm guilty."

"Josh I'm sorry about that."

"Mone you don't have anything to be sorry for. I never hid my feelings about you from her or anybody else. When she left me, I thought she would come back, but she didn't. That day I ran into you, I took that as a sign that we were meant to be together."

"I have a confession to make," Mone said shyly. "That night at the movies when Heidi walked up and wrapped her arms around you, I got jealous. I don't know why but I did. There I was standing next to my boyfriend getting upset because my ex-boyfriend was with his girlfriend. It took everything I had to keep smiling. You looked nothing like you looked when we were dating. When we were dating before, you were all skinny and nerdy looking." Cymone chuckled at the thought.

Josh laughed. "Damn, you really know how to make a brother feel good."

Mone smiled sheepishly. "Boy, you know you were tore up from the floor up back in them days."

"Mone, if I was so tore up, why were you with me?" Josh asked honestly.

Cymone turned to face Josh. "You weren't the most handsome boy, but the fact that you had a big heart and a great personality made you attractive to me."

Josh kissed Cymone on the back of her neck. "You need to go get in the bed so you can get some rest. If you keep laying here with me with your ass all pressed up against me like this something gone happen." Mone laughed and grinded her butt against him. Josh backed away from Mone. "You so dirty." Mone stood up and kissed Josh. She motioned for him to follow her. Cymone peeked in Laila's bedroom to see if she was snoring. When she heard her mother calling hogs, she knew she was out for the rest of the night. She led Josh to her bedroom, where they made love before saying goodnight.

The next morning, Josh and Cymone went to the police station to give their statements. Maurice was charged with two counts of aggravated assault with a deadly weapon and was being held without bond. The officer explained to them that Maurice would remain in jail until his court date.

On the way home, Cymone's cell phone rang. She looked at her caller ID but didn't recognize the number. "Hello."

Christi laughed. "I'm surprised you answered the phone."

"I started not to, but something said go ahead and answer it. You must got your number changed?" Cymone questioned.

"Yeah, I got a new phone." Christi replied nonchalantly.

"What's up with you?" Cymone asked knowing Christi had something juicy to tell.

"Tasha called me and said she heard some people talking about Maurice got arrested at Red Lobster last night." Cymone started crying. "Mone what's wrong?" Christi asked in a concerned tone.

Cymone said through sniffles. "Maurice did get arrested last night at Reb Lobster for trying to kill me."

"Oh my God! Mone, Are you okay?"

"Yes, I'm okay. If that police officer wasn't hungry and didn't pull up when he did, you would be reading about me and Josh in the paper. Christi, the hate I saw in his eyes was unbelievable. I haven't done anything to him but leave and not look back. Why does he hate me to the point he wants me dead?"

"Mone, you stood up to him. When shit got rough, you left and didn't look back. I may not have told you this, but I'm proud of you. It may have taken you a while to realize what type of person he was, but you removed yourself from that situation. Don't beat yourself up trying to figure out Maurice's crazy ass. If you feel like company, I'll stop by later on."

"I'd like that very much Christi."

"Ok, I'll bring some movies and popcorn, and we can have girls' night."

Cymone smiled. "Thanks, Christi. You have been a better friend to me than I have been to you. I promise I'll make that up to you."

"Mone that is water under the bridge, we can't go back and change the past. I've forgiven you, now all you have to do is forgive yourself. We can't keep dwelling on that. It happened, we got through it, and now we're better than ever. We gone look back on this when we're old and gray and laugh about it."

"Christi, you always know exactly what to say to make me feel better."

"Cymone, I almost forgot make sure you tell Ms. Laila she got to do her dance."

Cymone laughed. "No…please don't ask her to do that. She thinks she be looking good, and all she does is embarrass me."

"Girl, you know your mama can dance better than you and me both."

****

Maurice was finally given a court date. His lawyer explained to him that it would be in his best interest if he pled guilty. He told him that with the officer's testimony alone could get him a lot of time so Maurice stood in front of the judge and pled guilty to two counts of aggravated assault with a deadly weapon and received eight years. Cymone, Christi, Josh, Laila, and Tasha were all in the courtroom when he was sentenced. When a handcuffed Maurice was escorted out the courtroom, he saw Cymone. He smiled and mouthed, "They ain't gone hold me forever."

Josh looked at Cymone, who was visibly shaken. "Don't let him get to you."

When they walked out the courtroom, a tall brown skinned girl with a Halle Berry haircut walked up to Cymone. "Hey Cymone, can I talk to you for a minute?"

Cymone looked at her friends. "Give me a minute."

"We'll be in the car waiting for you," Christi said.

When everyone walked away, Cymone started talking. "You're the girl that was at Maurice's house that night I came over?"

"Yes, my name is Gina. That night when you came over I thought you wanted to fight me. When you said thank you and walked out I couldn't understand why you were thanking me. All he talked about was you. He talked about you so much I told him he should get back with you. He felt like I was being funny, and he beat me. Seeing him like that made me understand why you thanked me."

"I'm sorry you had to go through that with him," Cymone said sympathetically. "Maurice has a way of making you think he's the perfect guy. In the beginning, he was the best. There was no fussing or fighting. When I moved in with him, I became his property, and he felt like he had the right to dictate my life. I was so in love with him to the point I let him do it. I did everything he wanted me to

[116]

do whether I wanted to or not. I gave up my friends and my mom for him. I was always trying to make him happy. That night when I saw him with you opened my eyes. Maurice beat me within inches of my life. I laid in the hospital in a coma that he basically put me in, that he was responsible for, and not once did he visit or call to see how I was doing." Cymone shook her head, remembering all that she had been through.

"When I got out the hospital, he told me he would come see me and bring me something to eat. When I called him back that night, you answered his phone. I knew right then that Maurice didn't love me. My mom and my friends had been trying to warn me about him, but I didn't want to listen. God gave me a second chance at life, and I'm taking full advantage of it. I know he's not gonna be locked up forever so while he is, I'll live my life without looking over my shoulders."

"Cymone, I want to apologize to you," Gina said, with tears in her eyes.

"You don't owe me an apology."

"Yes, I do. That night when he followed you and your boyfriend to Red Lobster I knew what he was planning to do. I could have called you to warn you what was about to happen, but I didn't."

"Gina everything that happened that night was in God's plan. That officer was sent there to protect me that night. Even if you had called me and warned me about what he was planning to do, and we didn't go to Red Lobster that night, he would have just tried another day. He met his fate that night. Now you and I both can rest easy at night knowing he's where he deserves to be."

"Thanks, Cymone. If anything had of happened to you that night, it would have been on me. I can't shake this feeling of guilt, but I am so glad that you are okay!"

"You had nothing to do with it so don't feel that way. You're a victim just like me. We both fell for the lies he was dishing out." Looking at her watch, Cymone remembered that her friends were waiting on her. "Gina, I really have to be going. It was nice talking to you."

"Thanks for taking the time to talk to me." Gina watched as Cymone ran off to the car.

Chapter 12

"I think this day calls for a celebration. Maurice is behind bars for the next eight years. I have all of you here with me. Life can't get no better than this," Cymone was ready to celebrate.

Christi smirked. "Did you see the look on his face when they were escorting him out?"

"Dude is a straight up mental case," Laila said. "We will not have to worry about him for a while, I'm just glad my daughter wised up."

"Ma, you don't know how bad I wanted to talk to you about what was going on. I couldn't talk to Christi because we weren't speaking. I felt like I was in this world all alone. I didn't know what to do. He had me so messed up in the head I wasn't thinking clearly."

"You could have come to me Mone," Tasha said.

"You could have come to me too." Christi scolded. "I know we weren't on good terms, but I would have never turned my back on you."

"I picked up my phone to call you plenty of times, but I always hung up. I guess I was more ashamed than anything. I knew in my heart that you would never go behind me, but Maurice was all in my ear telling me it was you that took advantage of him." Just then Cymone's cell phone started ringing. When she looked at her caller ID, she didn't recognize the number, so she sent the call to voicemail. Her phone beeped indicating she had a new voicemail message. Cymone checked her messages and was flabbergasted by what she heard. She dropped her phone and ran out of the room crying.

Laila ran behind her. "What's wrong Mone?" She said in a panic.

Tasha and Christi followed to see what was going on. Mone was in her room lying on the bed crying. Laila sat down on the bed and rubbed Mone's back. "What's wrong? Who was that on the phone?"

Cymone rolled over. "Ma he's never gonna leave me alone."

"Was that Maurice who called you?"

"Yes, he told me that he may have to do eight years in prison, but when he get out he's gonna finish what he was about to do before he was so rudely interrupted by that officer."

"Did you save the message?" Christi chimed in. "I mean this nigga is really sick. He's on his way to prison, and he's calling threatening you."

Cymone moaned. "I just want to forget about it. I want to forget about him. Lord knows if I can turn back the hands of time I would have kept walking that day in Footlocker."

"Mone, you can't let him get away with harassing you!" Tasha was livid.

"I'll save the message, I'm pretty sure there will be plenty more. The police will need more than one message to call it harassment. I'm sorry if I'm ruining everybody's day." Cymone looked down with sad eyes. "That message just caught me off guard. I'm okay now. Josh should be on his way back. He just had to go home and get something. I'm gonna call him and see how much longer it'll be before he gets here." Cymone got off her bed and walked back into the living room to retrieve her phone. Josh answered the phone and quickly told Mone he was on his way out the door. Cymone heard a guy's voice in the background of their call say "I need to talk to you right quick."

"Mone, let me see what this dude want, and I'll be on my way." Josh said.

"Don't take too long. Maurice done called here threatening me already."

"That dude is sick for real. I'll be there before you know it."

"Okay, love you."

"Love you too Cymone."

Cymone hung up the phone and looked at Laila. "He'll be here in a minute. Some dude was at the door when he was leaving. I heard him say he needed to talk to Josh right quick."

"What did he say when you told him about Maurice?" Tasha asked.

"He just said dude is sick for real."

"I knew something was wrong with him that night he raped me," Christi added.

Cymone looked at Christi with pleading eyes. "I never gave you the chance to tell me what happened that night. If you don't mind, will you tell me everything that happened?"

Christi gave Mone a skeptical look. "Mone you sure you want to hear it?"

"Yes, I'm sure." Cymone said trying to smile. It would be hard, but this story needed to be heard. She needed to know the truth, and her friend deserved to be listened to.

Christi cleared her throat. "Well, after you passed out he helped you in the bed, and he gave me some cover and a pillow. I had way too much to drink so I was in the bathroom bent over the toilet for a while. I finally got comfortable enough to fall asleep. I was dreaming about T.I. and all of a sudden I started feeling good. I thought I was having a wet dream, but when I opened my eyes, Maurice was between my legs licking me like I was a Popsicle. I tried to get him off me, but he jumped on top of me and pressed all his weight down on me. I could hardly breathe so screaming was out the question. He was having sex with me like…like we were a couple or something. I thought he was gonna be rough with me, but he wasn't. He was moaning and telling me how good I felt. I was crying the entire time, but that didn't make him stop. Mone, the only thing that made me feel guilty about that night was the fact that I had an orgasm. I didn't want him or what he was doing to me, but my body betrayed me and he knew it. I guess that's why he was calling me asking me if we could get together again because he thought I wanted him."

Cymone grabbed Christi's hand. "You don't have a reason to feel guilty. I'm the one who should be feeling guilty. I should have known you wouldn't have done anything like that. Just then Cymone's cell phone rang, she didn't look at her caller ID she just answered the phone. "Hello. Yes, this is Cymone Jones. Who is this? Yes, I know Josh Hayes…. He's my boyfriend. What is this

[123]

about?" Everyone in the room got quiet as Cymone let out the most horrific scream.

"What's wrong?" Laila said in a panic. Cymone tried to speak, but she started hyperventilating instead.

Christi knelt down in front of Cymone and grabbed her hand. "Calm down Mone. Slow your breathing down before you pass out."

Tasha began rubbing Cymone's back in circular motions. Laila heard somebody saying hello and noticed somebody was still on Cymone's phone. Laila picked the phone up. "Who is this?" She was ready to go off, thinking it was Maurice.

The voice on the other end replied. "This is Officer Grant with Macon police department. We were called out to the home of Josh Hayes. His neighbors called 911 and said they heard yelling coming from his home and then a gunshot. They saw a black male running away from the home. When we arrived, we found Mr. Hayes lying on his living room floor with a gunshot wound to his chest."

Laila gasped and covered her mouth. "Is he okay officer? Please tell me he is okay."

"Sorry ma'am, but Mr. Hayes is deceased. His cellphone was lying on the floor beside him, so I dialed the last person that called him which was Cymone Jones."

"Yes officer, that's my daughter."

"She sounds pretty upset. Will you give her my condolences?"

"Yes, thank you Officer." Laila wrapped her arms around Mone. "Baby girl I'm so sorry."

"Mom who would do this to Josh? Josh never hurt nobody." Cymone was crying uncontrollably.

Christi and Tasha were speechless. They couldn't wrap their minds around what had just happened. Cymone's cell phone rang again. This time she looked at the caller ID and noticed it was the same number Maurice had called her from earlier. She looked up at Laila. "It's Maurice."

"Let it go to voicemail and see if he leaves a voicemail," Christi stated. Seconds' later Cymone's phone beeped indicating a new voicemail message. She called her voicemail and put it on speakerphone. Sure enough, he had left a message.

"Hey, Mone. How is that punk ass nigga you call your boyfriend doing? If and when you talk to him tell him I told him I wasn't that nigga to play with."

"Mone you got to call the police. He just told you he had something to do with what happened to Josh," Tasha stated.

[125]

"Tash, Maurice is locked up. How did he do something to Josh? Even if he did, it's gonna be hard proving considering he's locked up," Cymone cried. "Ma why would anybody want to hurt Josh?"

****

One week later, Josh was laid to rest. Everybody that was at his funeral spoke very highly of him. Christi even got up and sang her favorite song, "His Eyes are on the Sparrow." After she was finished, there wasn't a dry eye in the church. When they arrived at the burial site, the preacher spoke comforting words to the family.

As they lowered Josh's body into the ground, his mother who had been so strong finally broke down. She yelled out repeatedly. "God, why my baby?" Her family members had to restrain her in her seat. They feared she would fall on top of her only son's casket. Josh's mother was being escorted away but stopped short when she noticed Cymone. "My son loved you very much." She said through sniffles. "He talked about you even when the two of you were broken up. He just had told me a few days before he was killed that he wanted to ask you to marry him." Josh's mother broke down again. The thought of her only son being gone was too much for her. Cymone knew the pain she was feeling because she too felt the same pain.

Cymone wrapped her arms around Josh's mother and hugged her like her life depended on it. The two stood there hugging and crying on each other shoulders. It brought comfort to the both of them. Cymone pulled away and with tears in her eyes she said. "I'm here for you whenever you need me." Ms. Hayes patted Cymone's cheek lovingly. "Thank you baby." She said barely audible.

Cymone stayed at the grave site after everybody was gone. She needed to be alone with Josh for a little while. "Josh I miss you so much. I feel like we were cheated. I mean, we just reconnected. Then your mother just told me you wanted to marry me. I definitely would have married you Josh. You were, and still are, my hearts joy. You gave me that unconditional love that everybody is always searching for." Cymone wiped her eyes and took a deep breath before continuing. "I should have known something was about to happen the last time I talked to you. Since we've been together you have called me Mone or Babe, never Cymone. Before you hung up the phone, you called me Cymone." Trying to hold it together, she continued to speak to her lost love.

"Josh, I know I shouldn't question God, but I can't help but ask why you? Why did you have to go back home that day? Why couldn't you have just stayed with me? Why couldn't you have told that dude you didn't have time to talk because you had somewhere important to be? I promise you I'm gonna do everything I can to find out who did this to you. In my heart I know Maurice had something to do with it." Cymone felt a hand on her shoulder causing her to jump. She turned and looked up to find Nicholas, Maurice's old friend standing there. She wiped her tears away and cleared her throat. "Hey, Nicholas. What are you doing here?"

"I wanted to talk to you." Nicholas said extending his hand to help Cymone up.

Cymone took Nicholas hand and stood up. "Talk to me about what?" She asked brushing her skirt off. Before Nicholas could respond, Laila walked up.

"Mone are you ready to go?"

Nicholas looked at Laila then back at Cymone. "I'll get up with you later." He turned to walk away, offering up a weak smile before he excused himself.

As soon as Nicholas walked off Laila said. "Who was that?"

"That's Nicholas… Maurice's homeboy."

"What did he want with you?" Laila asked, still watching Nicholas.

With a confused look on her face, Cymone said. "I don't know he said he wanted to talk to me, but he didn't say about what. It's just strange because the whole time Maurice and I were together all he ever did was say hey to me. We have never held a conversation. So for him to want to talk to me about something is puzzling."

"Well, when you do talk to him, make sure you're not alone. Something's not right with him. I just can't put my finger on it. But anyways, Christi and Tasha wanted me to tell you they would be over to the house later. They wanted to go home and change clothes."

"Ma, I really just want to be alone today. I know they want to come over to keep my mind off Josh, but I want to think about him. I was extremely happy the entire time we were back together." Cymone stood there, smiling at the memories.

"Tasha and Christi knew Josh also. Why not share your feelings with them? I'm sure they won't mind talking about him for a few hours."

Cymone smiled. "Yeah, you right. I have two of the best people in the world as friends. How did I get so lucky?"

Nick sat in his car watching Cymone and Laila. He started his car up, but before he could put it in gear, his cell phone rang. "What up? Yeah, I tried to talk to her, but her mom walked up. I guess they're about to go home. She was crying when I approached her, but she's smiling now...Nah, the police don't have any leads, but the investigation still open. The only thing I've heard is his neighbors seen a man running from his house. Okay, yeah, I can do that." Nick disconnected the call and trailed behind Cymone and her mother, keeping his distance.

Laila and Cymone arrived home to find Christi was waiting in the driveway. Cymone got out of the car looking around. "Where's Tasha?"

"She said she would try to come by later. She wasn't feeling too good."

They walked inside the house, and Laila went straight to the kitchen to put the food on the table. She placed her hands on her hips. "It's so much food here I won't have to cook for a few days."

"Oh, you gone have to cook tomorrow because after today I'm not gonna want any more of this." Cymone replied.

Laila smirked. "If it's left up to me to cook tomorrow you'll starve. You gone have to cook for yourself."

Christi started laughing. "Ms. Laila you know Mone can't boil water. Mone, remember when you tried to fry chicken in water?"

Cymone and Laila burst out laughing. Cymone playfully hit Christi on the arm. "You wrong for that. I thought it was grease in the pan. I knew it didn't look right because when I placed the chicken in the pan it didn't sizzle." Cymone wagged her finger in front of Christi's face. "It was your fault."

Christi stopped laughing. "How was it my fault? I told you I had put the water on for the Mac&Cheese that you would have to put the grease on for the chicken."

Laila wrapped her arm around Cymone's shoulder. "My poor baby can't cook a lick."

"It's okay ma. I like your cooking anyway." Cymone said with a smirk.

Laila had placed all the food on the table. All they had to do was fix their plates. Once everybody was seated with their plates in front of them, Laila blessed the food.

"Josh would have enjoyed this, having all his favorites at one time. He would have been in food heaven." Cymone smiled at the thought.

"Josh could eat. For him to be so small, he could put away some food. Remember the cookout we had after graduation? Josh had three plates, one with all the meat, one with all the sides, and one with desserts." Christi and Cymone started laughing. "His mom started fussing at him, telling him his eyes were bigger than his belly. She didn't think he was gonna eat it all, but he did. He ate all that then wanted some more." Christi wiped a tear as they laughed about their friend.

They sat at the table for some time, finishing their dinner and reminiscing about Josh. After they were finished eating they retired to the living room where they continued talking about Josh for hours. Christi looked at her phone and noticed it was almost midnight. "Girl, it's late. I better be heading home."

Cymone placed her hand on Christi's knee. "Thank you, I really enjoyed sitting here talking with you about old times."

Christi smiled. "You don't have to thank me. I know you're dealing with a lot right now so if you need to talk to me at three o'clock in the morning or three o'clock in the afternoon call me. If you just want to scream and yell at somebody, call me." The girls stood and walked to the door. Before Christi opened the door, she turned to Mone and gave her a hug. "Take care and don't forget what I told you. Anytime you need to talk just call me."

"I will." Replied Cymone.

Chapter 13

It's been 2 months since Josh was laid to rest and Cymone was still trying to deal with the loss. It was hard to mourn his death when Maurice was constantly calling to harass her. Cymone walked into the kitchen and smiled. "I can't believe this. Are you okay?" She looked up at her mother Laila, smiling.

Laila looked at her daughter. "Oh, you got jokes this morning."

"Ma, I'm just saying, how many times in the last few years have you ever gotten up and cooked breakfast?" Cymone leaned over the counter and rested her chin in her hands. "I'll wait." She said sarcastically.

Laila swatted at Cymone with the spatula she held in her hand laughing. "It's a first time for everything. You just sit yo tale down and enjoy it."

Cymone surveyed the stove, noticing everything her mom had cooked. There were crispy strips of bacon, cheese grits, fluffy eggs, golden brown biscuits, stacks of pancakes, salmon patties and shredded hash browns. "Dang ma, you went all out." Cymone started licking her lips.

"I woke up this morning feeling good so I decided to cook. Christi and Tasha are supposed to be coming over to have breakfast with us." Laila said flipping the pancake.

Cymone kissed Laila on the cheek. "You're the best mom a girl could ever ask for." She grinned, stealing a piece of bacon.

"If you don't get your butt away from here stealing my bacon, I'm gonna go upside your head with this spatula for real!" Laila said, waving the spatula in the air.

Cymone bit the piece of bacon dramatically. "I'm gonna go shower and get dressed before Christi and Tasha get here."

Twenty minutes later Christi, Tasha, Cymone and Laila were all sitting to the table enjoying the buffet style breakfast Laila had prepared.

Ms. Laila you outdid yourself, everything was delicious. Thanks for inviting us." Christi said.

With a mouthful of pancakes, Tasha nodded her approval and thanks as well.

"You girls are more than welcomed. I'm glad you enjoyed it." Laila said sipping her coffee.

Cymone pushed her plate back and rubbed her stomach. "I think I ate too much." Just then she jumped up from the table and ran to the bathroom. Seconds later all you could hear was Cymone gagging viciously. Laila stood up to go check on Cymone but Christi got up and waved her off. "You finish your breakfast, I'll go check on her." Christi walked towards the bathroom worried, but Cymone was already coming out. "You okay?" Christi asked in a concerned tone.

With her hands on her stomach, Cymone leaned up against the wall. "I think I might be pregnant."

Christi hands flew to her mouth in shock. "OMG, are you serious?"

"I'm not sure, but there's a possibility I am. I thought I was late because I've been stressed and depressed. What if I have a little Josh growing inside of me?" Cymone felt herself beaming at the possibility of carrying Josh's baby.

Christi and Cymone walked back into the kitchen. Cymone could see worry written all over her mom's face. "I'm okay Ma." Cymone said sitting down. Laila couldn't understand why Cymone was smiling so hard after she had just been throwing up seconds ago.

Still smiling Cymone took a deep breath and said. "I might be pregnant."

Laila spit out the coffee she had just sipped. 'What?" She asked coughing a little.

Tasha sat there with a piece of bacon in her hand, frozen unable to say anything.

Christi and Cymone looked at each other and laughed at Tasha and Laila's reaction to her news.

"Ma, I haven't had my period in months. I thought it was because I was stressed and depressed about losing Josh, being pregnant never crossed my mind."

Laila stood up looking around frantically. "Where are my car keys?" She said rushing around the house. Laila found her keys and headed towards the door.

"Ma, where are you going?" Cymone asked in a panic.

"I'm going to the drugstore to buy a home pregnancy test." She said with a smile.

Cymone shook her head. "This woman bought to be all over me if I am."

Fifteen minutes later, Laila burst through the door with a bag full of home pregnancy tests. She was determined to get an answer. "Here you go," She said, handing Cymone the bag.

Cymone looked in the bag. "Dang Ma, why you buy so many?" Looking at all the boxes Cymone noticed they were all different. "You bought one of each kind." She shook her head, chuckling.

[137]

"I sure did, now go in the bathroom and take all of them. It's a cup and dropper in the bag also. Just pee in the cup and use the dropper to put the urine sample on all the test." Laila said shooing her daughter towards the bathroom.

Cymone got up and went into the bathroom with all her items. She did as her mother said and walked out of the bathroom. Laila jumped up and ran to her daughter. "What did they say?" She asked nervously.

"It takes three to five minutes to register a result." Cymone said sitting down on the sofa.

Everybody sat in silence waiting to find out if Cymone was going to bring another life into the world. So many thoughts ran through Cymone's mind as the minutes passed. She was happy and sad at the same time. Happy to bring Josh's baby into the world but sad knowing her son or daughter would never know their father. Tears weld up in Cymone eyes. She blinked rapidly, trying to keep them from falling. Christi was sitting beside Cymone, she reached for her hand and gave it a gentle squeeze. "It's gonna be okay." Christi said as if she were reading Cymone thoughts.

It's been more than five minutes, I know." Laila said.

Cymone turned to Christi, "Will you go look and see what the tests say?"

"Are you sure you want me to go?" Christi questioned.

"I'm sure." Cymone said.

Christi ran to the bathroom, moments later she screamed and ran back into the living room jumping up and down. "We're having a baby!" She said over and over in an excited tone. Cymone didn't move she stayed seated on the sofa. Tears streamed down her face like a waterfall. Laila got up and sat beside her daughter, she didn't say anything she just wrapped her arms around Cymone and hugged her. Tasha and Christi both joined in making it a group hug.

The next morning Laila took Cymone to the doctor. They found out she was 11 weeks. Cymone couldn't believe it, the reality of everything hadn't set in yet. "Ma, can we go by Josh mother's house? I want to tell her the news in person." Cymone asked gazing out the window.

"Sure baby." Laila responded, glancing at Cymone.

Cymone squeezed Laila's hand while ringing Ms. Hayes doorbell. Laila looked at her daughter. "It's gonna be okay." She said with a warm smile.

Ms. Hayes opened the door shocking Cymone and Laila by her appearance. Ms. Hayes had always been a heavy set lady who wore her weight well. Her hair and nails were always done and she dressed to perfection. The woman that stood in front of them looked nothing like her. This woman looked to be 80 years old, her hair was matted to her head, she looked like she hadn't bathed or changed clothes in months.

Brushing her hair back and suddenly feeling embarrassed, Ms. Hayes gathered herself. Her "Hey," was just above a whisper.

"May we come in?" Cymone felt herself fighting to keep her tears from falling.

Ms. Hayes stepped to the side allowing Laila and Cymone to enter her home.

"Ms. Hayes I apologize for just popping up over here. I have something I want to share with you and I didn't think telling you over the phone would be appropriate." Cymone said.

Ms. Hayes gestured for Laila and Cymone to have a seat on the sofa. "You don't have to apologize baby." Ms. Hayes said, slowly sitting down in the rocking chair.

Cymone sighed heavily and blurted out the news. "I'm pregnant."

Ms. Hayes sat there for a second trying to process what Cymone had just said to her. Once the realization of her words set in, Ms. Hayes hands flew to her mouth and tears began flowing from her eyes. Laila clasped her hands together in front of her face as if she were praying. Happiness, love and hope could now be seen in Ms. Hayes eyes and that warmed Laila's heart. She understood the pain Ms. Hayes was feeling because she too had lost her only son. Ms. Hayes stood up and walked over to Cymone. She sat on the other side of her and placed her hand on Cymone's stomach. "How far along are you?" She asked rubbing Cymone's stomach.

"I'm 11 weeks." Cymone proudly responded.

Ms. Hayes grabbed Cymone hands. "Thank you for giving me a reason to live. I promise to be here for you and the baby. Anything you need just let me know. I know Josh would have been right by your side so since he can't be here, I'll be here." Ms. Hayes looked around as if seeing for the first time, feeling her sons' presence in the joyous moment.

"You don't have to thank me. I'm just glad I could give you something to look forward to. I apologize for not coming by to check on you." Cymone could no longer stop the tears in her eyes.

"Don't you do that." Ms. Hayes said wiping Cymone tears away. "You called and talked to me more than that Heidi girl did. Her and my son dated for years and not once did she call to see how I was doing nor did she come to his funeral. You have nothing to apologize for. Ms. Hayes spoke matter-of-factly.

Laila stood up letting Cymone know she was ready to leave. "Martha we will keep you informed on doctor appointments and everything dealing with the baby."

Cymone stood up wondering why her mother was all of a sudden ready to leave. "Ms. Hayes my next appointment is in three weeks if you'll like to go."

"I'll like that very much, thank you." Martha said.

Martha walked Laila and Cymone to the door and watched them until they pulled off. She closed and locked her door and returned to her rocking chair feeling like she had been given a second chance at life.

"Ma, why were you so ready to leave all of a sudden?" Cymone asked.

"I started thinking about Jarvis." Laila replied somberly. Cymone nodded and the ride was silent the rest of the way back.

Once back at home, Cymone went straight to her room. It had been an emotional day and she just needed to lie down and rest. Everything was happening so fast, in a few months she would be somebody's mother. The thought of raising a baby by herself was starting to weigh heavy on her mind. Cymone rubbed her still flat stomach and smiled. "I wonder who you're gonna look and act like? Will you look like your daddy and have my personality or will you look like me and have your daddy personality? Either way it goes you are gonna be a pretty awesome kid just like your parents, especially your daddy. I promise to tell you all about him when you're old enough to understand." Cymone spoke lovingly to her unborn baby.

The next several weeks flew by fast. Before they knew it, Cymone and her support team were all in the doctor office, waiting to find out the sex of the baby. Martha seemed to be more excited than anyone else. She had kept her promise, and was at every doctor's appointment with Cymone. The woman that opened the door for Cymone and Laila that day had disappeared, and the real Ms. Hayes had returned. Her nurse walked in the room and was surprised by all the people that were gathered around Cymone. "Hey, I see you brought everybody with you today." The nurse walked in with a nervous smile.

Cymone didn't respond, she just smiled right back. She was just ready to get everything over with. The nurse poured cold gel on Cymone's belly and rubbed the wand over it. Moments later something appeared on the monitor. The nurse turned the volume up on the monitor and everybody gasped in delight. The baby's heartbeat was loud and strong.

"Wow, whatever you're having has a strong heartbeat." Martha gleamed, admiring her grandbaby on the monitor.

"What are you hoping for Ms. Jones?" The nurse asked Cymone.

"I just want a healthy baby." Cymone replied honestly.

"Okay Ms. Jones I want you to look right here." The nurse said pointing at a spot on the monitor. "Do you know what you're looking at? The nurse asked.

Laila hands flew to her mouth. "Oh my God, it's a boy!" She squealed.

Cymone looked at the nurse to see if what her mother had just said was correct. Seeing the smile on her face confirmed it, she was having a boy.

"Congratulations Ms. Jones, you are having a healthy baby boy." The nurse said wiping the gel off Cymone stomach.

Cymone couldn't respond, she just lay there crying tears of joy. Christi was happy for her friend but the fact that she had loss her own son made her sad. Christi stepped out the room while everybody congratulated Cymone. Tasha noticed Christi leave and figured she needed a little time to herself.

Chapter 14

The day had finally arrived. Cymone was in the hospital about to give birth to her son. The last few months had been rough on her. She developed pre-eclampsia and was put on bed rest for the remainder of her pregnancy. Cymone lay in her hospital bed in excruciating pain. Laila placed a cold, wet rag on her daughter forehead. Martha held her hand and Tasha and Christi rubbed her feet. They were all trying to make Cymone as comfortable as possible.

"Mommy it hurts so bad!" Cymone screamed out in pain, writhing in the hospital bed.

"I know baby but it's almost over." Laila said.

Just as Cymone started straining the nurse and doctor walked into the room. The nurse noticed Cymone pushing and urged her to stop. The doctor pushed Cymone legs apart. "Don't push sweetie, try to relax." She said in a calm, soothing voice. Laila and Martha both abandoned Cymone to witness the birth of their grandson. Tasha and Christi moved back a little to let the grandparents have front row seat.

"Ms. Jones when I say push I want you to give me a big push." The doctor said. Cymone nodded but didn't say anything, she was in too much pain to talk. The doctor felt

Cymone stomach tighten up. "Push Cymone." Cymone pressed her chin in her chest and bared down as hard as she could. "That's it Cymone, you're doing great, just one more push." Cymone repeated her actions and was rewarded by the sounds of her crying baby.

"Congratulations Ms. Jones, you did well!" The doctor was encouraging, patting her on the leg. "Who wants the honors of cutting the umbilical cord?" Dr. Gordon said holding up the scissors. Laila looked at Martha with tears in her eyes. "You can have the honors Martha."

Martha grabbed the scissors from Dr. Gordon. "Cut right here." Dr. Gordon said showing Martha where to cut. Tears filled Martha eyes and her hand trembled as she cut the cord where the doctor had instructed. Once the cord was cut the nurse scooped the baby up and placed him in the bed to be fixed up. She cleaned him up, wrapped him in a blanket and placed a blue knitted hat on his head. Laila, Martha, Tasha and Christi stood and watched everything the nurse did to the baby.

"Can I see him?" Cymone asked feeling left out. Everybody was fussing over the baby and she had yet to lay eyes on him. The nurse picked the baby up, walked over to Cymone and placed the beautiful bundle in her arms. The moment Cymone laid eyes on her son, it was love at first sight. She held him close to her and whispered, "I love you" over and over again.

"Congrats Mone, he's perfect." Christi said.

Cymone beamed with excitement. "Thank you, he looks just like Josh." She said as tears escaped her eyes.

"Yes he does." Martha added. Looking at her grandson took her back to the day Josh was born. It was like he had been reincarnated.

"What are you naming him?" Laila asked rubbing her grandson head.

Cymone looked at Martha. If it's okay with you, I would like to name him after Josh."

Martha was already crying, and to hear Cymone say she wanted to name the baby after Josh made her cry harder. "I would love it if you named him after Josh." Martha said through her sobs.

"Joshua O'Neil Hayes, Jr." Cymone said kissing her baby on the forehead.

***

"Christi are you okay?" Tasha asked her friend.

"I'm okay, why you ask that?" Christi replied.

"You have been acting kind of strange ever since we left the hospital."

Christi sighed heavily. "I'm okay, I guess I'm just missing my son. I didn't get the chance to hear my baby cry. Cymone will be able to take her baby home and spoil him. I left the hospital empty handed." Christi said with tears welding up in her eyes.

Tasha pulled her friend in for a hug. "I'm sorry Chris."

Christi pulled away from Tasha and wiped her eyes. "You don't have to apologize. I think about my son all the time. I know in the beginning I didn't want him because of how he was conceived but I grew to love and want him. I don't question God's decision to take him from me; I just try to accept it."

Christi's phone began to vibrate in her pocket. She removed the phone from her pocket and sighed at who was calling. Tasha looked at her friend curiously. Christi took a deep breath. "Hey Mone... How you doing?" She asked trying to sound upbeat.

"Come off it Chris, you don't have to pretend with me. What's going on?" Cymone said.

Christi smiled and shook her head. She should have known regardless how much she tried to hide her feelings, her friend Cymone would pick up on it.

"Mone, I'm okay. It was just seeing your son made me think about the son I lost. I got a little emotional and decided to leave. I didn't want to rain on your parade." Christi said, truthfully.

"Chris, you have been my friend for years. I turned my back on you and you have still been here for me. I don't know how you feel, I can only imagine the hurt and pain you feel on a regular basis but please don't feel you have to avoid me. Let me be here for you like you have always been there for me. I want you to be Josh's godmother. I know he can never replace your son but he can fill that emptiness you feel."

Tears welled up in Christi eyes. "Are you sure you want me to be his godmother?" She asked, in a shaky voice.

"I'm absolutely sure; I mean who else would I ask to take on such an important job?" Cymone said with a chuckle.

Everything was falling into place. Josh had the best grandparents a baby could ever ask for, a godmother who acted like a second mother and Tasha, who took on the role of auntie. Cymone thought life couldn't get any better. The first year of Josh life was the best. Being able to watch him grow up and learn new things always intrigued Cymone.

The little things, like him holding his own bottle, or sitting up by himself brought joy to her life. She often wondered how Josh and little Josh would have interacted with each other.

***

Two years had passed and there still wasn't a lead in Josh's murder. Nick watched the news and kept his ear to the streets trying to see what all the police knew. He knew the neighbors saw him running out of the house, but he had his back turned to them, so they didn't see his face. He didn't remember seeing anybody else on the block that day, but who's to say nobody else saw him. Since the family was pressuring the police department to keep the investigation open, the police had put up a $10,000 reward for any information regarding his death.

Nick felt like he was in prison. He walked around a free man, but he was constantly looking over his shoulders wondering if today would be the day the police arrested him. Then to make matters even worse, Maurice called every day wanting to know what Cymone was doing. Was she seeing anybody else? Did she look sad? Nick didn't know how he would break the news to Maurice that Cymone had had a baby, especially by Josh. Every time Nick saw Cymone and her son, the guilt ate him up inside.

[151]

Knowing that he was the reason that Cymone's little boy had to grow up without a father crushed him. Now, Maurice wouldn't stop bugging him about the whole situation. "Maurice, I'm not following Cymone around anymore, I mean if she gets with somebody else, you can't be mad about it. She wasn't your girl before you got locked up." Nick spoke in an agitated tone.

"Nigga, I ain't trying to hear that shit from you. Cymone will always be my girl. I told her if I couldn't have her no other nigga would, and I meant that shit. These crackers can't hold me forever. They gave me eight years, and I've done two. My lawyer told me it was a good chance I could be out in three years."

"What you planning on doing when you get out?" Nick asked curiously.

Maurice sucked his teeth. "I'm gonna finish what I started."

Nick shook his head in disgust. "Dude something is seriously wrong with you. This girl has moved on with her life, and yo dumb ass locked the fuck up thinking about her every day. Do you think she's thinking about you? You done already did two years, and you say you can get out in three years. Now you talking about adding more time on. If you get out and do what you keep saying you're gonna do,

[152]

that's life with no parole. I refuse to let you take me down with you, so after today there's no need to call me." Nick stated, matter-of-factly.

Maurice started laughing. "Nigga, you think you just gone cut me off like that? Nigga, it ain't gone happen. You out there on the streets because I need you to be. Remember there's no statute of limitation on murder. One phone call and your ass will be in here with me."

Nick became furious. "There's no evidence linking me to that. It'll be your word against mine. Who do you think they'll believe?" He chuckled knowing Maurice's word wouldn't mean squat.

"Yeah, but video evidence is always better than an eye witness." Maurice said cockily. "I had to make sure you would follow through with it, so I got somebody to follow you. They recorded you running out the house with the gun still in your hand."

Nick couldn't believe what he was hearing. He should've known it was a matter of time before Maurice pulled some bullshit like this. "Are you serious? You gone try to blackmail me just so I will keep doing your dirty work? Go ahead and do it then. You won't have to worry about getting out in three years." Nick threatened.

[153]

"Nick there's nothing linking me to Josh's murder. I was already locked up when he was killed. How would I have something to do with it?" Maurice was smirking uncontrollably.

Nick was so pissed that he just disconnected the call.

When Maurice heard the dial tone, he bursted out laughing. "Nigga's fall for anything." Maurice didn't have a video of Nick running out the house, he just told him that so he wouldn't go running his mouth. He walked back to his cell and laid on his bed. He had a picture of Cymone hanging on his wall. The thought of making her pay for leaving him was what kept him going. Thinking of ways to hurt her made time fly by. He had been calling her every other day for two years, and not once had she answered his calls. He wrote her letters and not once did she respond back. Maurice thought to himself that once he touched down, she was gonna wish she had of answered his calls or responded to his letters.

Taking Josh away from her is not all he had planned for her. He planned on taking everybody she loved away from her. Maurice couldn't understand why he couldn't let Cymone go. She was the only girl who had walked away from him and that made him feel some type of way. In his own twisted way, he really loved Cymone. He just had a fucked up way of showing it.

That night she caught Gina at his house, he saw something in her eyes he had never seen before. It was like she was no longer afraid of him, and that made him angry. As long as she was afraid of him he knew she would never leave him, but that night she grew some balls and left. Maurice grew tired of just thinking about Cymone, so he decided to try his luck and call her again. He dialed her number and to his surprise she picked up on the second ring. Maurice was so shocked that she had answered, he didn't know what to say. Cymone said hello three times and just as she was about to hang up the phone Maurice shouted, "Hey Mone. I didn't think you would pick up. I've called you and written you letters for years, and you've never responded." There was a long moment of silence. "How have you been?" He said, in a nervous tone.

Cymone sighed deeply. "Maurice, what do you want?"

"I just wanted to see how you were doing." Maurice replied.

Cymone was nonchalant in her response. "Let's see, you pointed a gun at me. You threatened to kill me. You had my boyfriend murdered. You've been calling me for years, harassing me, threatening me some more. You got Nicholas following me watching my every move. How the fuck you think I'm doing, Maurice?"

Maurice was shocked. He didn't know she knew Nicholas was following her. He hesitated before speaking again, trying not to sound surprised. "I'm not harassing you Mone. Regardless of what happened in the past, I do love you."

Cymone shouted. "Yeah, you love me so much you beat me within inches of my life and lied to the paramedics saying you found me like that. Love isn't supposed to hurt Maurice. The night I moved in with you, you changed. The sweet guy who opened doors for me and wrote me notes just to say I love you? Gone. The guy who would rub my feet and plant soft kisses all over my face? Disappeared. The guy who would never go to bed without calling me just to say good night? Vanished. Where did he go? What happened to that man? I was left to deal with the monster you had become. When I moved on with my life with Josh, you hated it and took him from me." Cymone said sobbing.

"Mone I had nothing to do with that." Maurice said faking sincerity.

Cymone laughed. "You can say that until you're blue in the face. Maybe if you keep repeating it, you'll start believing it yourself. I know you had something to do with it. Look, Maurice, I have to go. I would really appreciate it if you wouldn't call me anymore."

"Mone, wait, before you hang up. I just want you to know that I'm sorry for everything. Maybe one day you will be able to find it in your heart to forgive me."

Before Mone disconnected the call, Maurice heard a little voice in the background. "Mommy, why you crying?"

Maurice frowned in confusion. "Did I just hear what I thought I heard?" He said dialing Cymone's number again. "Answer the phone Cymone." Maurice boomed through gritted teeth. He dialed Cymone's number repeatedly but she didn't answer. Maurice became furious. He hung up and dialed Nicholas. Maurice didn't give him the time to say hello before he went off. "Did Cymone have a baby?"

Nick didn't know what to say, and honestly he had no idea how Maurice had found out. "What are you talking about?" Nick stuttered.

Maurice was so mad, spittle flew from his mouth as she spoke. "Don't fucking play with me. You know exactly what I'm talking about. Why didn't you tell me Mone had a baby? Don't sit here and say you didn't know." Maurice was pacing, infuriated.

Nick didn't want to confirm what Maurice felt he already knew so he simply hung up the phone. That was a situation he wanted nothing to do with. He already felt guilty for taking Josh life, he didn't want to be responsible for Cymone's life as well. There was no telling what Maurice would do to Cymone if he knew for sure she had a baby. Hell, there was no telling what he would do to the baby.

Maurice didn't bother trying to call Nick back, he already knew he wouldn't answer the phone. Maurice went back to his cell feeling like his world had come to an end. Nick never mentioned seeing Cymone with another man and he damn sure hadn't mentioned a baby. Maurice didn't want to think about Cymone possibly having a baby so he turned his radio on and lay back on his bed. 'Half on a Baby' by the ingenious R. Kelly started playing. Maurice grabbed the radio and threw it against the wall. Unfortunately for Maurice the radio kept playing the song. He grabbed his pillow and covered his head trying to drown it out.

Chapter 15

Cymone was going through her things and found an old picture of her and Josh. It had been two years since he was killed, and it still felt like it happened yesterday. Cymone refused to date anybody else. A part of her died with Josh but having her son gave her a piece of him back. She knew she should be out living life. Josh would have wanted that for her, but she just couldn't bring herself to do it. Just then she heard the doorbell ring. She wasn't expecting anybody else. Marth had already picked JJ up so she rushed to the door to see who was ringing the doorbell. Before she opened the door, she looked out the peephole and saw a tall brown skinned guy wearing a UPS suit. She opened the door and was greeted by the warmest smile she had ever seen.

"Good evening, ma'am I have a package for Laila Jones." Cymone just stood there staring at the man. The UPS worker cleared his throat. "Ma'am, I just need your signature."

Cymone shook her head and smiled. "I'm sorry where do you need me to sign?" The UPS worker handed her his clipboard along with his pen and showed her where to sign. Their fingers lingered together as she returned his pen and board. He fumbled around for a moment, handed her the package, and told her to have a good day.

"You do the same." She was mesmerized by the gorgeous man standing in front of her.

Cymone couldn't keep her eyes off of him. She was totally mesmerized. This guy was all kinds of fine and the uniform just enhanced his physique. Cymone hurried and placed the package on the floor and ran outside before the UPS guy could pull off. "I don't normally do anything like this, but it's something about you. If I give you my number will you promise to call?" She stared at him, out of breath.

The UPS worker smiled. "I can do that." He handed her his pen and the clipboard she had just signed her name on. Cymone wrote down her number and gave the clipboard back to him. She turned and walked away. She stopped and turned to face him.

"What's your name?"

The guy smiled. "I'm Todd." Cymone turned and ran back to the house grinning from ear to ear. She didn't know what came over her; she had never been that bold before. When she walked inside, she heard the house phone ringing. She didn't even bother to look at the caller ID she just picked the phone up. "Hello."

"Why aren't you answering your cell?" Christi said.

"I was outside giving my number to the UPS guy that just delivered a package here."

Christi let out an exasperated breath. "Yeah right, you gave your number to a guy that just delivered a package to your house. Tell that shit to somebody else."

"Seriously, I just gave my number to the UPS guy. His name is Todd, and he's so freaking fine."

Christi started laughing. "Go head then girl."

"I was nervous, but I was like what the hell, he's either interested or not."

"What does he look like?" Christi asked.

"He has to be about 6'4, slim build, brown skinned, his eyes are mesmerizing they're like a hazel brown, but his smile is what got me."

"I'm happy for you. Maybe he'll be the guy to help you raise JJ." Christi said excited for her friend.

"He just might be the one Christi." Cymone said thinking about the possibility.

"Mone, have you seen or talked to Tasha?" Christi said, snapping Cymone out of her thoughts.

"No, I've hardly talked to her lately. When I call her, she's busy. It's always she'll call back, but she never does. After like the third time she did it, I said I wasn't calling her anymore. When she wants to talk, she'll call."

"She does the same thing to me, but it's strange because she has never done that before. When we were going through our little storm, she was always around. If I called, regardless what she was doing, she would always talk. She came by every day to check on me, now it's like she don't want to be bothered." Christi said.

"Tasha has been acting distant since Josh was killed. I never said anything because we were all grieving in our own little way. It puzzled me because she hardly knew him, but she took his death just as hard as we did if not harder. Remember she was supposed to come over after the funeral, but she never showed up," Cymone replied.

"Yeah, I remember that. I went by to see her the next day, and she said she wasn't feeling good." Christi stated.

"I don't mean to change the subject, but how about Maurice called here today." Cymone said dryly.

"What did he want?" Christi asked, shocked that Cymone was talking about Maurice.

"He's been calling like every day and sending me letters. I felt like if I talked to him he would stop calling so much. He apologized but denied he had something to do with Josh's murder. JJ walked in the room and asked me why I was crying right before I hung up. I know he heard

[162]

him because he kept calling back but I didn't answer again."

"That dude is mental for real. When he get out he better not bring that psycho shit around my baby or we're gonna have more problems." Christi spat, meaning every word. "I'm so glad you made it out of that situation with your life."

"Chris, I almost didn't make it out. I look back and ask myself, how could you be so stupid? I believed him when he said he would never hit me again. I had never been in a situation like that before, and I didn't know what to do. I had nobody to turn to."

"Mone you had people to turn to, you just chose not to. Regardless of how you felt about me, I still considered you my friend. I was on the phone with Tasha that day you were rushed to the hospital. All of a sudden I just got this feeling like something was wrong with you. I called your phone, and Maurice told me you were in surgery. My heart dropped to my knees when he told me that."

"Ma told me you were there every day talking to me. Sometimes I could hear people talking, but I couldn't make out voices. I owe you so much Christi. You were there for me in my time of need, and when you had your miscarriage, I was nowhere around."

[163]

"I've told you that's water under the bridge. We can't go back and change that."

"Do you still think about the baby?" Cymone asked.

"Every day, I was torn in the beginning because of how he was conceived. I don't believe in abortion, so I knew I would give birth to him. I had planned on giving him up for adoption, but the more I felt him moving inside me, the more I wanted to meet him. I didn't know what to do Mone, so I prayed and gave it to God. He knew what was best for me, and I don't question his decision. I'm just grateful I got a chance to hold him in my arms."

"Did you give him a name?"

"Yeah, I named him Christian Alexander Parker."

Cymone smiled before saying, "You named him after your dad?"

Christi giggled. "Can you believe that? I actually named my baby after the man that left me when I was a baby and never looked back, but that's an entirely different conversation. Girl, I've taken up enough of your time, so I'll catch up with you later."

"You make sure you do that, and if the UPS guy calls, I'll make sure to call you to give you the 411."

The girls said their goodbyes and disconnected the call. Cymone felt better at that moment than she had in years. She decided she would get out of the house and treat herself to a Mani/Pedi.

Tasha lay in her bed crying. Lately, that's all she seemed to do. For the past few years, she has been dealing with some personal issues. Tasha wanted to confide in her friends, she just didn't know how to. She was afraid of how they would treat her if they found out. It all started when she went to South Carolina to visit her relatives. While she was there, she met this guy that swept her off her feet. He was every woman's dream, tall and handsome with some gorgeous eyes. He had the most captivating smile. It was lust at first sight. The entire two weeks she spent in South Carolina was spent with him. He took her out to eat, to the movies and bowling. Tasha had so much fun she didn't want to go home. The night before she left they made love. It was the best sex Tasha had ever had. It was the kind of sex that made you want to call and tell your mom about. The guy she met promised that he would keep in touch. He also promised to visit her in Macon. The guy stood true to his word. He called and texted every day. Three weeks after leaving South Carolina he was in town for a visit. He only stayed for the weekend, but it was the best weekend ever.

She wanted to share her joy with Cymone and Christi but she could never find the right time to share it. The day they buried Josh she was supposed to go over

Cymone's house, but she made up an excuse not to go because her boo called and said he was in town. Tasha felt bad for not being there for Cymone, but she didn't want to sit around and be sad all day. She knew Cymone would be doing a lot of crying, so she chose to be happy and sexually satisfied with her boo.

The relationship went on for two years, but the last few months of their relationship Tasha noticed a change in him. He would still call and text, but the visits became less and less. Tasha felt like he was seeing somebody else, but he kept assuring her that she was the only one. He told her his new job had him all over the place, and he just wasn't able to make those trips like he once could. Tasha wanted to believe him, but in her heart she knew the relationship was coming to an end. The day her doctor called her to come into the office confirmed the fact that the relationship was over.

Tasha had been faithful. She was so in love with her boo that sexing another nigga was never on her mind. When she started itching and had a little discharge, she thought that maybe she had a yeast infection. So she made an appointment to see her gynecologist, and a week later she went back to get her results. She found out that what she thought was a yeast infection was really gonorrhea and chlamydia. She was shocked, and thought she was crazy. How the hell you get two STD's at once? Tasha sat in her doctor's office feeling humiliated and dirty, but that was just the tip of the iceberg. Her doctor explained that if his patients test positive for any STD's, he always tested for HIV. Tasha's eyes bucked.

The doctor sat Tasha down and held her hand. "I'm sorry to have to inform you, but your test came back positive for the virus."

Tasha felt like a ton of bricks were sitting on her chest. She couldn't breathe. She could see the doctor lips moving, and she could hear him, but what he was saying sounded like the cartoon characters on Charlie Brown. She stood up and attempted to walk out of the office, but her legs had a mind of their own. She took one step and fell.

Tasha was startled by her ringing phone. She looked at her caller ID and noticed it was Christi calling. She let it go to voicemail. She didn't feel like talking. She waited to see if her phone would beep indicating she had a new voicemail, but instead it began ringing again. This time it wasn't Christi. This call was coming from an 803 area code. She picked up on the third ring.

"What do you want?" She spat nastily.

"Damn is it like that? I'm in town and I wanted to know if I could stop by and see you."

"Nigga you got some nerve calling me asking me that shit. Hell no you can't come by here. You have ruined my life, and you sit around and act like shit okay."

"Look, I don't know what you talking about, I'm good. I went to the doctor, and I'm clean. You need to take that up with the nigga that gave you that shit because it wasn't me."

"I'm not even about to argue with you. I know you were the only person I was sleeping with. Before you, I had never had an STD. So fuck you nigga!" Tasha disconnected the call. "The nerve of this nigga." She jumped when she heard a knock at the door. She got up and walked to the door saying to herself, "I know damn well this nigga ain't just pop up at my house after I told him not to." She swung the door open and was about to give him the business, but stopped when she looked in Christi's face.

"Oh bitch, you'll answer the door, but not your phone." Christi said walking past Tasha not waiting to be invited in.

Tasha closed the door and sarcastically said, "Well come on in Christi."

"Tasha why haven't you been answering or returning my calls?" Christi looked around the room.

"Chris, I've been a little under the weather and haven't felt like talking."

"Bullshit Tash, tell that shit to somebody who don't know you. What's going on with you? You were there for me when I was going through that shit with Mone, and you were there for me when I went through my miscarriage. Why won't you let me be here for you?"

Tasha tried to keep the tears from falling but soon lost the battle. Christi pulled her friend to her and held her tightly. Tasha collapsed in Christi arms and cried like a newborn baby.

"Let it out Tash, let it all out. I'm here for you." Christi said rubbing Tasha back lovingly.

They stood in the middle of the living room in an embrace that seemed to last forever. Tasha finally pulled away and sat down on the sofa. Looking at her friend with concern in her eyes, Christi took a seat as well. Tasha wiped her tears with the back of her hand.

"I'm not gonna beat around the bush with you. I'm just gonna come right out with it." Tasha took a deep breath and blurted out. "I'm HIV positive."

Christi sat there for a minute trying to register what Tasha had just said. It sounded like she said she was HIV positive but Christi knew that wasn't what she meant. It couldn't be what she just said. Tasha could tell Christi was trying to process the news; she sat with a blank stare. "Christi are you gonna say something?" Tasha asked trying to snap Christi out of her thoughts.

Christi shook her head in utter disbelief. "How long have you known?" Christi asked, still in shock.

"I've known for a while now." Tasha offered.

"Why haven't you been told me?" Christi questioned.

"I didn't know how. I thought after you found out you wouldn't want to hang out with me or be around me in fear of contracting the virus."

Christi grabbed Tasha hands and looked directly in her eyes. "I'm not dumb. I know holding your hands or hugging you and being around you is not gonna infect me. I wish you would have come to me. I could have been here with you helping you cope with the news. Look at yourself Tash, you've lost mad weight." Christi said trying to hold back her emotions. "This Tasha that I'm looking at is not my vibrant friend. Yes, you have HIV, don't let HIV have you. Don't stop living your life because of this. If you don't mind me asking. Who gave it to you?"

"You don't know him. I met him the time I went to South Carolina."

Christi looked at Tasha. "That's been damn near three years ago. You mean to tell me you were seeing somebody and didn't tell us?" Christi asked with a frown. "Damn Tash, that's cold."

Christi shifted in her seat to get a better look at her friend. "That's why you've been so distant with us? Me and Mone were talking about you, but we thought it had something to do with Josh. After his funeral, you started acting kind of strange."

"The day of the funeral when I was supposed to go to Mone's house and didn't? It was because he was in town."

"Are you still with him?" Christi asked hoping the answer was no.

"Hell no. This nigga act like he ain't got shit. He called here a little while ago asking if he could come over. He ruined my life Chris. He was the only person I was sleeping with and he kept telling me I was the only one. I believed him. I mean I had no reason not to. He was everything I ever wanted in a man. He was handsome, smart, funny, and attentive. When we were together, it was all about me. He was the open doors, hold hands type of guy." Tasha stated.

"He sounds like a great guy." Christi replied.

"I thought so too until he infected me with HIV. I asked him where he got it from and he swore almighty God that I must have gotten it from somebody else because he was clean. It's like he's in denial about the whole thing."

"Could you have gotten it from somebody else?" Christi asked with raised eyebrows.

"No, I've been tested before, and it always came back negative. I don't sleep around like everybody think I do, and whenever I do have sex, I always use protection. I even used protection with the fucker that gave me this shit. It's just after being with him for a while I didn't feel the need to use them anymore. That was the biggest mistake of my life. Chris, you wanna know the sad part about all of this?"

"What's that?"

"I still love the son of a bitch. I was tempted to let him come over here today, but I stood my ground and told him no."

"Have you told your mom?"

"Yeah I told her and she wants nothing to do with me. She said she didn't want me there anymore because I might infect her and Latrice."

Christi gasped. "Are you serious?"

"Yeah, that's why I got my own spot."

"I'm sorry you went through this alone, but you know you didn't have to."

"After my mom turned her back on me, I felt like you and Mone would do the same thing."

"Tash I'm not trying to be funny, but you need to go shower and put some clothes on." Christi said, fanning her nose.

Tasha smelled under her arms and frowned. "I do smell a little tart."

Christi laughed. "Yes you do, now go. After you get dressed, we're gonna go get something to eat because you look like you haven't eaten in days. We're gonna shop and just hang out. You need to get out this house and grab your life back. I don't know who this person is in front of me. I want my friend back." Christi playfully pushed Tasha's arm. "Now go introduce yourself to Mr. Shower. I'm sure he'll be happy to be reunited with you."

Tasha punched Christi in the arm. "You wrong for that."

Christi grabbed her arm. "No, you wrong for that," Christi replied, pointing at her appearance.

Tasha laughed for the first time in weeks. She felt guilty for thinking Christi would turn her back on her. Tasha showered and did her hair. She had to admit, that hot shower gave her life. When she walked into her living room, Christi had cleaned up.

"Girl, you didn't have to clean up my mess," Tasha frowned, looking around her now clean living room.

"I know I didn't have to, I just wanted to change the mood in here. The clutter was too depressing."

"Thanks, girl. Well, I'm all ready to go. How do I look?"

Christi gave her the once over and said nonchalantly. "You clean up nice, but what happened to the baggy jeans and t-shirt?"

"I decided to switch things up a little." Tasha strutted past Christi in her white leggings, mint green silk looking shirt that hung off her shoulders and some mint green sandals. "You know I look good."

Christi rolled her eyes. "Whatever bitch."

Chapter 16

When Laila walked in the house, Cymone ran to her and gave her a big hug. Laila looked at her daughter trying to figure out what was different about her. "Girl what's wrong with you?"

"Nothing ma I'm just happy to see you."

"Yeah right, what's going on? What's got you all happy?"

"You got a package from UPS today."

Laila looked confused. "How did getting a package from UPS for me make you so happy?"

Cymone smiled. "It wasn't the package. It was the guy that delivered the package. Ma he was so fine. I ran and gave him my number before he left."

"What? You mean to tell me my quiet, sometimes shy girl, made a move on a cute guy?" Laila smiled despite her best efforts to be serious. Maybe she could finally stop worrying about her baby.

"Yep, I sure did. I think it's time to start dating. I mean I'm twenty-two with a baby and all I do is spend time around the house. I'm tired of watching life pass me by." Cymone twirled on her toes, spinning around the kitchen.

"Good for you baby girl, you deserve to be happy. I know going through that shit with Maurice and then losing Josh took a toll on you. I admire you for being strong for JJ through it all. Speaking of JJ, where is my munchkin?" Laila asked looking around for him.

"Mrs. Martha came and picked him up."

"That woman love herself some JJ." Laila plopped down on the sofa. "Tell me about this guy who has put this big ass smile on your face."

Cymone grinned sheepishly. "Ma, he's tall, brown skinned, he has hazel brown eyes and a smile to die for. His name is Todd, and I don't want to get too happy because he hasn't called yet."

"Oh, don't worry he'll call. I didn't raise any ugly kids."

"I know that's right because my brother was one handsome man."

Laila smiled. "Yes, he was."

"Ma, I miss him so much. He was over protective of me, but I could go to him about anything and he never once judged me. I wish he was here to meet JJ, and guide him."

"I miss him too baby girl. He was my first born and my only son. I lost my baby because some dude got his ass tore up and decided he wanted to shoot up the place."

[177]

"Ma, when are we gonna celebrate the 4th of July again?"

"I don't know if I'll ever celebrate that day again." Laila gazed out the window.

"I understand that's a painful day for you. It's painful for me too, but we always celebrated, and I believe Jarvis would want us to continue. That way we won't be mourning his death, but celebrating his life. You know Jarvis loved a good cookout."

Laila continued to stare off into space. "You right about that, he loved grilled food."

"The 4th is coming up next month, and that will mark the 7th anniversary of his passing."

"I guess we could invite a few people over and celebrate his life instead of walking around mourning him." Laila perked up at the thought of a celebration. It was time for change.

****

Maurice lay in his cell thinking about Cymone. In the last two weeks, he received four letters, all from Gina confessing her love for him. He was happy to hear from her and pleased that she still wanted to be with him, but he would be lying if he said he felt the same way. While reading the letters from Gina, he silently wished they were from Cymone. He wished it had been Cymone confessing her love for him instead of Gina. He also received a letter from his lawyer saying that it was a possibility that he could be released next month. He didn't want to get his hopes up, but hearing the news had him feeling better than he had the whole two years he's been there. He was ready to get up out of that hell hole, but he didn't know if he could live in the same city as Cymone and not try to be with her. He knew he fucked up time and time again, but being behind bars gave him time to think about the pain he caused the people who loved him.

Maurice told his counselor when he was a child his father beat him and his mother every day, so that became the norm in his house. He explained to her that he grew up thinking that's how you showed love. Talking with the prison counselor twice a week gave him the leverage he needed to manipulate her. He convinced her that he understood what his father did was wrong and what he was doing was also wrong. The counselor explained to him that if he wanted to have a healthy relationship he would need to break the cycle. He would need to ask for forgiveness from the people he hurt and then start forgiving himself.

He knew Gina wasn't the woman he wanted to be with, but he would settle down with her and treat her better than he had in the past. He knew in his heart Cymone would never take him back, and he had nobody to blame, but himself. He decided to write her a letter apologizing for everything he had done to her and prayed that one day she would find it in her heart to forgive him.

****

Todd contemplated calling Cymone. He thought she was the most beautiful girl he had ever seen. He was feeling her, and he knew she was feeling him because she couldn't keep her eyes off of him. He appreciated a woman who knew what she wanted, and it seemed like she wanted him. He was surprised when she ran out to the truck and gave him her number.

Todd picked up his cell and called Cymone. The phone rang five times and just when he was about to hang up she answered. "Hey Cymone, this Todd. You gave me your number."

Cymone smiled. "I remember you... UPS guy right?"

"Yeah, that's me."

"I was beginning to think you wasn't gonna call."

"Why would you think that?"

"It's been two weeks since I gave you my number and you just now calling me."

Todd laughed. "I didn't want you to think I was desperate."

"Yeah, any excuse is better than nothing at all."

Todd and Cymone talked like they had known each other for years. They spent well over an hour on the phone just getting to know each other. They found out they had a lot in common. They both were huge Tupac fans who didn't believe he was really dead. They both thought Kanye West was an attention seeker, and they both liked 90's R&B music. Cymone made sure she told Todd about her son. That way it was up to him if he wanted to continue getting to know her. To her surprise, he was okay with it. He explained to her that he loved kids and would love to meet her son one day. Cymone invited Todd to the cookout on the 4th of July, and he gladly accepted. When Cymone got off the phone with Todd, she ran to Laila's room and dove on her bed looking like the cat that ate the canary.

"Girl, what is wrong with you?" Laila said.

Cymone couldn't hold in her excitement any longer. "He called Ma. We have so much in common. That was our first official conversation, and it felt like we've known each other for years. The conversation just flowed. He knows about JJ and he still wants to get to know me better. I invited him to the cookout, and he agreed to come, so you'll get the chance to meet him."

Laila chuckled. "I'm ready to meet the guy that got you feeling all happy go lucky."

"Have you invited any of your friends over? I know they gone be shocked when you tell them you doing something for the 4th."

Laila cut her eye at Cymone. "I haven't invited anybody yet. I told Pat about it. I'm just not feeling it. I know I told you we would celebrate this year but to be honest with you, I'm not really up to it."

Cymone popped her lips. "Do you want me to just cancel the plans?"

Laila saw the disappointment in her baby girl's face. "Mone I know how much this means to you, you don't have to cancel the plans. I said we would celebrate, and that's what we're gonna do."

Cymone tried to hide her excitement. "Ma if you really don't want to I'll understand. Jarvis was your firstborn and your only son, and he was taken away from you. I hear you some nights crying for him. When it first happened, I felt like you loved him more than me." Cymone held her hand up before Laila could speak. "Wait a minute Ma, let me finish before you say anything. I know

[182]

you love me, but after Jarvis was killed it was like a part of you died with him. I was here with you feeling your pain and you treated me like I wasn't even here. Christi used to say, that's your mom, you know she loves you just give her time to grieve the death of her son. I gave you your space. I tried to be the perfect daughter. I kept the house clean, I cooked, I got good grades, and I wasn't in the streets like most teenagers. I just felt like all of that went unnoticed. When I got with Maurice, that's when you started coming around being Ma again, but for so many years before then I felt neglected by you."

"Mone, I'm so sorry you felt that way. Losing Jarvis devastated me to the tenth power. I didn't know how to cope. I was here physically, but mentally I had checked out. Trust me the things that you did, they didn't go unnoticed. I thanked God for you every night. When I came home from work the house was always clean, dinner was done, and you didn't ask for much. I'm sorry you felt neglected because that's not what it was. I appreciated you because you didn't have to take on that responsibility. Baby girl, I love you with all my heart. There's nothing I wouldn't do for you. I will walk over hot coals barefoot to protect you. Hell, I was ready to commit my first homicide

[183]

when that no good ass Maurice put you in the hospital. I lost one child to violence; I refuse to lose another one."

"Ma, can I ask you a question?"

"Sure, what's on your mind?" Laila replied.

"What happened between you and daddy? He has been a constant no show in our lives since I can remember."

"Your father decided one day he didn't want to be a daddy anymore. It was a package deal with him. When I no longer wanted to be in a relationship with him he no longer wanted to be daddy. That man cheated, lied and beat me."

Cymone was shocked. "Daddy beat you?"

"Yes Mone, your father used to hit me. He would go hang out half the night with his homeboys, and I guess the chick he was out creeping with wouldn't act right, so he would come home and take it out on me. I stayed with him for you and your brother's sake. I wanted the two of you to have a mother and father at home."

"Ma, that wasn't a reason to stay with him."

"I know that now, but at the time I felt like it would benefit you and Jarvis to have both of us at home. The night he came home drunk and mad for no reason and beat Jarvis, I knew then I had to go. I would sit back and take the beatings from him, but when he started directing his anger towards y'all I lost it. When I packed our stuff and left, I never looked back. I thought I wouldn't be able to take care of two kids and a household alone, but God made a way for me. I ended up getting a promotion at work, and when Grandma died, she left me one of her insurance policies. That money really came in handy. It gave me that cushion I needed."

Cymone walked over to her mom and wrapped her arms around her. "Ma, I'm proud of you. You took care of us all by yourself. We never went lacking for anything. You was always there for us even if you were tired. I'm glad God picked you to be our ma. I know Jarvis felt the same way. I mean he was a mama's boy."

Laila smiled. "That he was. Mone enough about that, I'm looking forward to the festivities. Your Uncle Mike said he was gonna try to make it."

"Uncle Mike is coming? I know we gone party like it's 1999." Cymone hopped up, moving and grooving.

"You already know how my brother gets down."

"Ma don't remind me. Lord, I feel sorry for Ms. Pat. Every time Uncle Mike come visit he always hitting on her."

"I think we should do something special in remembrance of Jarvis."

"That would be nice, Ma. See you're slowly warming up to it."

Chapter 17

It was 2:00 in the morning and Cymone couldn't sleep. There was nothing on TV she could watch to make her fall asleep. JJ was still at Martha's house. She knew Tasha and Christi were asleep, so she didn't bother to call either of them. When she was on her way to the kitchen to get something to drink, her cell phone rang. When she answered Todd immediately started talking.

"Did I wake you?"

Cymone smiled. "No, you didn't wake me. I can't sleep. I was just about to get something to drink from the kitchen."

"What are you doing up so late?" Todd leaned back, ready to talk to Cymone. Just the thought of her made him grin.

"I never sleep at night. I'm always up."

"I'm usually asleep, but for some strange reason sleep can't seem to find me tonight. Do you want some company?" Todd asked.

"Are you volunteering?"

"Only if you want me to." Todd's grin returned.

"You know where I live then. I'll see you when you get here." Cymone hung up the phone and smiled to herself. She couldn't believe she was entertaining another man. It was just something about Todd that had her open to the idea of loving again. Talking to him was easy. He was a great listener. The conversation was never dull and boring. He had a way of making her feel like nobody else existed in the world but the two of them.

When Todd arrived at Cymone's, she decided they should sit outside in the backyard. Cymone looked up in the sky. "The full moon is beautiful and bright tonight."

"It's not near as beautiful as you are."

Cymone bumped Todd's arm with her elbow. "Flattery will get you a long way in life."

"I'm not trying to flatter you, I'm just speaking the obvious. Can I ask you a question, beautiful?"

"Sure, go ahead."

"Why are you single?"

Cymone sighed. "My boyfriend was killed a little over two years ago. After he passed I found out I was pregnant. My ex-boyfriend is in prison for trying to kill me. As you can see, my track record with men has not been all that great."

"Damn… What did you do to your ex?"

"I left him and didn't look back. My ex was really abusive towards me. He beat me so bad one night I thought

[188]

I was gonna die. It took me a minute to realize I could do better without him, but I've got it figured out now."

"Is that why you walk with a limp?" After noticing the pained expression on Cymone face, Todd felt bad for the words that came out of his mouth. "I'm sorry, I didn't mean to get to personal."

Cymone waved him off. "You don't have to apologize, I've accepted my limp. The night I thought I was gonna die he stomped me which led to some broken ribs, a punctured lung, and a broken hip."

Todd shook his head in disgust. "Dude was straight up stupid for putting his hands on you. Women are supposed to be loved and cherished, not abused and misused."

"Why don't you have a girlfriend?" Cymone was curious, and wanted to change the topic. Maurice couldn't ruin this moment, not now.

"I haven't found the right one. The last girl I dated did the unthinkable. She contracted something from the dude she saw behind my back, and she kept trying to say she got it from me. I went to the doctor to get checked, and I came back clean."

"Damn that's messed up." Cymone felt herself wanting to ask what his ex thought she had contracted from him.

"Enough about our past relationships, let's talk about where we going with this. I like you Cymone, and I really wanna get to know you better."

Todd and Cymone sat outside for hours. When the sun started coming up, Cymone knew it was bedtime.

Todd looked at the sunrise in disbelief. "Damn, I didn't mean to keep you up all night."

"You don't have to apologize, I really enjoyed myself. Talking to you feels so natural. It's like we've been friends forever."

"Can I see you later?"

"Sure, I'm not doing anything."

"Great, I'm gonna let you get some sleep, and I'll call you later." Todd kissed Cymone on her forehead and left.

Cymone had no problems falling asleep. When her head hit the pillow, she was out like a light. When Cymone finally woke up it was after 3 pm. She couldn't believe she had slept that long. She checked her phone and saw she had six missed calls and a few text messages. Noticing a text from Todd, she hurried and opened it. It read. "I hope you slept good beautiful when you get a chance call me. I would like to take you out to dinner and maybe bowling if you're down for it." Cymone grinned and said to herself, "Hell yeah I'm down with it." She texted him back and told him she was down and to let her know when he wanted to leave so she could be ready. Cymone returned Christi's phone call.

"Damn you just decided to call me back." Christi said when she answered.

"I'm sorry chick, but I just woke up."

"Mone it's after 3:00. You never sleep this late." Christi gasped in astonishment.

"I know, but I didn't go to bed until 7:30 this morning."

"Why were you up so late?"

"I couldn't sleep last night, and I knew you and Tasha were asleep. Todd called me, and I told him I couldn't sleep so he came over. We sat outside all night and talked."

"Are you sure that's all y'all did?" Christi was not so easily convinced. "You on this phone sounding all in love and shit."

"Girl stop. He didn't even try to kiss me. He ended up kissing me on my forehead before he left. I had a text from him when I got up. He wants to take me out to eat and bowling."

"Did you tell him you would go?"

"Yes, I did but I need to call Martha to see if she's keeping JJ or bringing him home.

"Good for you girl you deserve to be happy. If she brings him home you know I don't mind keeping my baby. When are you gonna let me and Tasha meet him?"

"He's coming to the cookout on the 4th so you and Tasha will get to meet him then. I know you guys will like him, I mean he's been nothing but a perfect gentleman. Our conversations are the best. It's like we've known each other for years, not weeks."

"Call me and let me know if I need to keep JJ."

"I will. What did you want when you called?"

"Oh, it was nothing. I just wanted to have breakfast with my bestie this morning."

"Aw... I feel bad now. I'll make it up to you I promise."

"I know you will Mone. I'm gonna let you go so you can get yourself all dolled up for your date."

"I'll call you as soon as I talk to Martha."

****

Todd picked Cymone up at 8:00 on the dot. They agreed on Margarita's for dinner and drinks. They made it to Margarita's and once they were seated they both ordered a large Mango Margarita. Todd wanted his drink on the rocks and Cymone asked for hers to be frozen. The waitress told them she would give them a few minutes to decide on what they wanted to eat. Cymone picked up her menu and scanned the choices.

She looked up from her menu smiling. "Everything sounds so good, I don't know what to choose."

"I usually get the house special," Todd offered.

When the waitress approached the table to take their orders, Todd looked at Cymone and asked if he could order for the both of them. Cymone didn't protest. Todd turned his attention to the waitress. "We'll have the house special." The waitress jotted down their orders and removed the menus from the table.

Cymone looked around in awe. "I've never been here before. I kind of like the romantic vibe in here."

Todd was about to speak but was interrupted by the waitress placing their drinks on the table. Cymone began rubbing her earlobe while looking at the monstrous drink that sat in front of her.

[193]

Todd noticed how Mone was looking. "Is everything okay?"

Cymone looked up from her drink with an uncertain look on her face. "I didn't know a large was gonna be this big. I'm not gonna be able to finish all of this."

Todd chuckled. "Is that what's wrong? You don't have to drink the whole thing Mone, just drink what you can." Cymone burst out laughing which made Todd start laughing. Todd shook his head. "I wish you could have seen the look on your face when the waitress sat that drink in front of you." The two sipped on their drinks and talked until the waitress brought their food out.

Cymone looked down at her plate. "This looks so delicious."

Taking a bite of his food, Todd grinned. "It tastes delicious too."

After they finished their meal they headed to Gold Cup for some bowling. Cymone explained to Todd that she had never been bowling before, so he had to take it easy on her. Todd and Cymone bowled for hours. He couldn't tell she didn't know what she was doing, considering the fact that she beat him four games to one.

Todd took Mone home, and they sat in his car for a while making out. Things had gotten so hot and heavy between them Cymone had to back away. Todd looked worried. "Did I do something wrong?"

Cymone started rubbing her earlobe again. "No, you didn't do anything wrong." Barely above a whisper Cymone continued. "Todd I really like you, but this is too soon."

Todd nodded in agreement. "I completely understand. I apologize if I crossed a line with you."

"No need for apologies, I enjoyed the kiss. I just want to get to know you a little better before we become intimate."

"I completely understand." Looking down at the bulge in his pants Todd smiled sheepishly. "I better let you go in the house."

Cymone smiled. "You still coming by on the 4th?"

"Yes… I wouldn't miss it for anything."

"Good, I look forward to you meeting my family and friends." Cymone gave Todd one more gentle kiss on the lips before getting out of the car. Todd waited until she was in the house before he pulled off. As soon as she was inside she called Christi and told her all about her date with Todd.

****

The 4th of July had finally arrived, and Cymone was ecstatic. She was so happy her mother had decided to go through with the cookout. Her Uncle Mike came up from Florida to celebrate with them. He even agreed to cook the meat. Christi and Tasha were on their way over. Tasha had told Cymone she wanted to talk to her about something important. Cymone hadn't talked to Todd, so she didn't know if he was gonna make it or not.

The day was turning out to be a wonderful day. The sun was shining, the grill was smoking, good music was playing, and the family was there. Cymone walked outside to see if Uncle Mike needed anything and was greeted by an unexpected guest. She locked eyes with him and frowned. It was like all of a sudden she had a bad taste in her mouth.

He walked up to her. "Hey, baby girl. How you been?"

"Only my mother is allowed to call me baby girl. It's Cymone to you." She replied nastily.

"I guess I deserved that."

"What are you doing here? I mean who even invited you?" Cymone looked around, frowning.

Before he could respond, Laila stepped outside, smiling. "I see you made it."

Cymone looked at her mother, puzzled. "You invited him here?"

"Yes Mone, I invited your father to be here today to celebrate our son's life."

Cymone looked at her parents, shook her head and went back inside the house.

"She really hates me, doesn't she?" Steve asked.

"Laila put her hands on her hips. "What do you expect from her? You haven't been here for her. Our daughter is grown with a son of her own. When was the last time you talked to her or even seen her? While she was laid up in the hospital in a coma not once did you visit her."

Steve was frustrated. "I know. I didn't come over here for this Laila. I know I wasn't there, and I can't go back and change it. I can only try to be here now." Then the reality of what Laila said sank in. "What you mean son of her own?"

Laila sighed knowing they were wrong for not telling Steve he had a grandson. "Yes, Mone has a two year old son."

"Mone had a baby and nobody called and told me? And y'all wonder why I'm not around!" Steve ranted, more hurt than anything.

"Calm down, it's not like you've been in contact with us. Laila hissed.

Just then Martha showed up with JJ. "Nana!" JJ squealed, running to Laila, reaching for her to pick him up.

"Hey my Munchkin... Did you have fun with Grandma Martha?" Laila smothered her grandson, planting kisses all over his face.

"Yes." He said laughing, fighting her but secretly enjoying his Nana kisses.

Steve stood there in awe at the sight of his grandson. Laila turned JJ so he was facing Steve. "JJ this is your grandpa Steve. Can you tell him hello?"

JJ laid his head on Laila's shoulder, pretending to be shy.

***

Cymone picked the house phone up to call Christi, but as she was dialing she heard somebody saying hello. Cymone looked at the phone. "Hello."

"Hey girl, I was just trying to call you."

"Where the hell are you?"

"At Tasha's house waiting on her slow ass to get dressed."

"Y'all need to get here like ASAP. My sperm donor is outside with my mother."

[198]

"What? Is Mr. Steve over there? I haven't seen him in years. Is he still fine?" Christi boldly asked.

Cymone rolled her eyes. "For real Christi."

"Girl, you know yo daddy was fine as hell. Why you think all of us wanted to stay at your house when we were little?"

"Whatever. Is everything okay with Tasha? She said she had something important to talk to me about."

"Mone, that's a conversation you're gonna have to have with Tasha. Speaking of the devil, she just came out of the bathroom, so I guess we're on the way. Don't run Mr. Steve off before we get there."

Cymone didn't respond, she just hung up the phone. When she turned around, she jumped and placed her hand over her heart. "You scared me."

Steve smiled. "I didn't mean to scare you. Can we sit and talk for a minute?"

"I really don't have anything to say to you."

"Cymone, I haven't been there for you, so I'm sure you have plenty to say. Give your old man a few minutes of your time."

"Okay, you have until Christi and Tash get here. Chris drives fast, so you better make it quick."

"First, I want to apologize for not being here like I should have been. I haven't always been a good person. I was a terrible husband and a lousy father. I can sit here and try to sugarcoat things for you, but what would be the point? You're a grown woman now with a handsome son of your own."

Cymone looked at Steve, trying to figure out how he knew she had a son.

Steve smiled. "He's oustide. Cymone, I'm gonna keep it real with you. Your mom and I were young when we had Jarvis. I thought I was ready to be a father and a husband, but I wasn't. In the beginning, things were okay, but not being able to hang out with my boys started problems with me and your mom. She had matured and was handling motherhood well. Me on the other hand, I was very immature and selfish. After you came along shit just went downhill. Don't get me wrong, I loved you and your brother. I just wasn't mentally ready to be a full-time daddy. Laila started hounding me about never being home. It was like the more she yelled and complained the more I stayed away from home."

"Ma said you use to beat her."

Steve put his head down in shame. "I'm not proud of that."

Cymone said. "You don't owe me anything. I don't need an explanation. Ma was there when you weren't and she never once complained. She always made sure Jarvis, and I was taken care of. Food was always on the table. The bills were paid. Regardless how tired she was she always made sure we ate dinner as a family. My mom worked her fingers to the bone to provide for us. She went without a lot to make sure we never did. She didn't get food stamps or welfare. She didn't even try to get child support from you. She never called and asked you for anything. I understand now that the relationship y'all had ended, I get that, but regardless of what went on between you and her you had two kids you left behind. Jarvis and I had nothing to do with what y'all had going on. Even if you couldn't have been there financially you could have been here mentally, physically, and emotionally. Did you ever once stop to think that I may have needed you?"

Cymone could feel herself getting emotional, but these were things she had been waiting a lifetime to say. He needed to hear her out. "Things got rough after Jarvis died. Did you come around to see if we needed help?"

Steve looked up and tried to answer but Cymone cut him off. "I'm twenty-two years old, and this is my first time laying eyes on you since I was fifteen. Do you know

[201]

what I've gone through since then? I was beaten within an inch of my life. The doctors put me in a medically induce coma because my body was in so much pain they told me I wouldn't have been able to cope. I have a permanent limp now. The guy that beat me is in prison, not for beating me, but because he pulled out a gun and was about to kill me and my boyfriend. Well, he succeeded in killing my boyfriend just not that night. He proved to me that he was telling the truth when he said if he couldn't have me, nobody else would. Josh has been gone for two years now. I have a son that will never get to meet his daddy and I miss him so much."

Cymone took a deep breath of relief. It felt good to get it out. "You don't even know me." She glared at her father. She hoped he at least felt guilty for abandoning her and her family.

Steve held his head down in shame. "I didn't know. There's no excuse. I should have been there for you. If it's not too late now, will you let me be there for you and my grandson? I know we can't get those years back. I'm a better man and father, I know I can be an even better grandfather. I would be honored if you would give me the chance to make things up to you." Steve begged for a second chance.

Cymone stood in front of her father with tears in her eyes. "I need you to be consistent in my life. Don't call and come by for a few days then fall off the face of the earth again."

With so much compassion in his voice Steve promised his little girl. "I'm gonna be here for you... I promise. I'm gonna make this up to you."

Just then Christi and Tasha walked in the house. Steve wiped Cymone's eyes, kissed her on the forehead and told her he loved her. That made Cymone smile. Steve spoke to Christi and Tasha on his way out back.

Christi smiled. "It's good seeing you again Mr. Steve."

Tasha looked at Cymone with a shocked expression. "That's your dad?"

"Girl ain't he fine?" Christi replied.

Cymone gave Christi a dirty look. Christi started laughing. "Don't kill me girl I'm just playing. The guy on the grill looks familiar. Who is he?" Christi asked.

"That's my Uncle Mike from Florida."

"Oh yeah, I remember him. He's always hitting on my mama when he in town."

"Where is Ms. Pat? Is she coming?" Cymone asked.

"She said she was coming. I guess she home trying to get dolled up."

Cymone turned to Tasha. "What is it you wanted to talk to me about?"

Before Tasha could respond the door opened and in walked Todd. Cymone smiled. "You made it. Come in let me introduce you to my girls. Tasha, Chris this is Todd. Chris this is the guy I told you about. When Tasha looked up and saw Todd standing there with his arm around Cymone, she lost it. She ran out of the house crying. Todd stood there looking like he didn't know what was going on.

He said with no emotions. "What's wrong with your friend?"

"I don't know. Have a seat. I'll be right back." Cymone and Christi ran out the house behind Tasha. They found her sitting in her car crying. "Open the door Tasha." Christi asked in a calm voice. Tasha hesitated but decided to open the door. "What's wrong? Why you run out like that?" Cymone asked in a concerned tone.

"Mone have you slept with him?" Tasha asked not making eye contact with Cymone.

Cymone looked confused. "Have I slept with who?"

"Todd. Have you slept with Todd?" Tasha said raising her voice.

"No, I just met him a few weeks ago. We've talked over the phone and went out to dinner and bowling. All we've done is kiss. What is this about Tasha?"

Tasha looked at Christi. "That's the guy I was telling you about." Christi covered her mouth in shock.

Cymone looked from Tasha to Christi. "Did I miss something? What's going on?"

"Mone I'm HIV positive, and the guy that's in your house is the one that gave it to me."

Cymone felt like she was about to faint. The universe shifted on its axis and knocked her down in the process. Cymone's breathing became erratic and tears streamed down her face. She looked at Tasha with hurt and confusion written all over face. "What, what did you say?"

Tasha felt so bad. She could tell by the way she looked at Todd she was really feeling him. She had no idea the guy she had told Christi about was Todd, and she definitely had no idea Todd was here, chasing after Cymone. This was such a mess. Tasha cleared her throat before she spoke. "A few years ago when I was in South Carolina visiting my family I met Todd. We kicked it the entire time I was there and when I came back home he started visiting me on the weekends. The day Josh was buried I was supposed to come over here and didn't, it was

[205]

because he had called and said he was in town. I went to the doctor because I thought I had a yeast infection, but it was gonorrhea and chlamydia. Then the doctor told me I was HIV positive. Todd was the only person I was with, and when I confronted him, he acted like he didn't know what I was talking about. He told me he was clean that I must have gotten it from somebody else, but I know it was him."

Cymone stood there in disbelief. She just stared at Tasha. She grabbed Tasha's hand and pulled her out of the car. She wrapped her arms around her and held her tight. She whispered in her ear. "I'm so sorry Tash. You must have been the ex he was telling me about. He said you was sleeping around on him and tried to accuse him of giving you something. He never said what it was, and I never asked."

"This shit is crazy. Who would have thought that your knight in shining armor would be Tasha's worst nightmare?" Christi stated.

Cymone walked back inside the house. She found Todd sitting in the living room watching TV. He looked up and smiled. "Is your friend okay?"

Cymone just looked at him. She couldn't believe he was sitting there all calm acting like he didn't know who

Tasha was. Cymone said as calmly as she could, "Is there anything you wanna tell me?"

Todd put the TV remote back on the coffee table. When he turned to look at Cymone, he noticed the menacing look she had on her face. He hesitated. "What do I need to tell you?"

Cymone folded her arms across her chest and started tapping her foot. "Well, for starters maybe you should tell me you're HIV positive. Then maybe you can explain to me the reason you acted like you didn't know who Tasha was."

Todd stood up. "Look, I don't know what your friend told you, but I don't have HIV. I've told her that several times, but she keeps insisting I'm the one that gave it to her. As far as Tasha goes, I didn't know she was your friend. I didn't want to embarrass you by letting you know I had fucked your friend."

"Even though she ran out of here in tears, you didn't feel the need to inform me about your relationship with her? You really fooled me Todd. I thought this was gonna be the start of something special."

"It still can be." Todd pleaded.

Cymone rolled her eyes. "Are you serious? You were sleeping with my best friend and gave her not only gonorrhea and chlamydia but HIV, and you think there's a chance for us. I don't fuck behind my friends and I most definitely will not fuck you knowing you got that shit. Somebody got to be looking out for me because I just dodged a death sentence."

Todd raised his voice. "How many times I gotta say I ain't got no damn HIV. Yo homegirl needs to get in touch with the nigga that gave her that shit because it ain't me. I've told her this a million times."

"Are you in denial or are you just nasty like that?" Before Todd had the chance to respond, Nick walked in.

"Hey, Mone. Your mom told me I could come on in." Cymone looked at Nick confused, and it must have shown on her face. "I need to talk to you about something, and I didn't want to discuss it over the phone. I can come back. I see you have company."

Before he could turn to leave, Cymone grabbed him. " No Nick, stay, Todd was just leaving."

When Nick heard Todd's name, he really looked at the guy that was standing there. Nick walked over to Todd. "Are you the Todd from South Carolina that drives a UPS truck?"

"Yeah, that's me. Why?"

"Do you know a chick named Teresa?"

Todd smirked. "Yeah, I know her. Why?"

"You were dating her for a minute, right?

"Damn Bruh... What is this ask Todd a million damn questions day? Yeah I know Teresa. We kicked it for a minute. What's it to you? Is she your bitch now or something?"

Nick balled up his fist and said through gritted teeth. "Nawl, she's my little sister."

Cymone heard the anger in Nick's voice and saw how his demeanor had changed. She stepped in front of him. "Nick you good? What's wrong?"

Nick looked down at Cymone. "I'm good."

Todd frowned. "You sitting here looking like you ready to fight because I fucked your sister?"

Nick shook his head. "Nawl, nigga you fucking my sister ain't shit. You giving her HIV is what got me heated."

Cymone couldn't believe what she was hearing. She looked at Todd and shook her head. "Are you gonna keep saying it ain't true?"

Todd didn't say anything, he just walked out. Cymone turned to Nick. "I'm sorry to hear that about your sister. Damn, I guess the saying is true. Everything that look good ain't always good for you. Just looking at him you wouldn't think he had that shit. Damn, I dodged a bullet for real. Nick, what did you want to talk to me about?"

"I got a call from Maurice and he said something about he may be getting out sooner than what he thought."

"How soon?" Cymone asked.

"Like before the end of the month soon. He also kept questioning me about whether you had a child or not." Nick looked concerned.

"I figured Maurice heard JJ that day he called. JJ walked in the room and asked why I was crying right before I hung up the phone. He kept calling back but I didn't answer."

"Oh, I was wondering why he asked me that out of the blue. He got back with Gina, so you don't have to worry about him. I just felt like you had the right to know. I didn't want you to be surprised one day you out and see him. He sounds like he gone get out and do good. He's been seeing a counselor who has been helping him with his issues."

"I wish him the best," Cymone replied. "He wrote me a letter apologizing for the things he did, but that went in one ear and out the other. He's apologized to me before, and I thought he was being sincere. The best thing we can do is stay away from each other. I pray Gina finds happiness with him."

"Mone, I'm gonna get up out of here and let you enjoy the rest of your day. I just wanted to give you the heads up on Maurice."

"Nick I appreciate you for telling me. My only concern right now is my son. I'm not gonna stop living my life because he's getting out."

Nick gave Cymone a hug and left. He walked out feeling guilty, despite giving her the warning she deserved. He promised himself that one day he would sit Mone down and tell her the truth. He just hoped she would be able to forgive him.

Chapter 18

Cymone thought the day would be a day of celebration, but all she's gotten all day was bad news. When she went outside to join her family, Uncle Mike was through cooking, and Laila had set all the food on the tables. Ms. Pat had made it, and Uncle Mike was doing what he always did when she came around. Everybody seemed to be having a good time.

Christi looked at Cymone with concerned eyes. "You good Mone?" She mouthed.

"Yeah, I'm good. Today has been one of those days. I find out the guy I thought could possibly be the one, used to date one of my best friends and Teresa. Not only did he date them, but he gave them both HIV. Then on top of that Nick tells me Maurice might be getting out before the end of the month."

Christi stood there speechless. She didn't know what to say.

Cymone smiled. "You looking like how I'm feeling."

Laila held JJ in one arm and waved her other hand over her head. "Can I have everyone's attention please?" Everybody stopped doing what they were doing and gave

Laila their undivided attention. "As you all know, on this day seven years ago, my son Jarvis was taken away from me. After his death, instead of celebrating on the 4th of July, I mourned the death of my son. My daughter Cymone told me that I needed to start back celebrating because that's what Jarvis would have wanted. Those of you that knew him knew he loved to have cookouts. He loved to celebrate all holidays, but the 4th of July was his favorite. That's why this year instead of mourning Jarvis we're gonna celebrate him. I know this is what he would have wanted."

Laila pressed play on the CD player and R. Kelly's 'I believe I can fly' started playing. Laila grabbed the seven white balloons that were tied to the table. One for every year Jarvis had been gone. She kept two, giving one of them to JJ. Laila handed two to Steve and Cymone and she gave the last one to Uncle Mike. They stood there together as a family holding the balloons thinking about their beloved Jarvis.

At that moment, Cymone cried for Jarvis and Josh. She missed them both so much. While R. Kelly was singing "I believe I can fly, I believe I can touch the sky. I think about it every night and day, spread my wings and fly away," they let the balloons go in remembrance of Jarvis.

[213]

One white balloon for every year he had been gone. Laila was crying, but this year they were tears of joy, not sorrow.

Maurice was parked across the street from Cymone's house, watching her and her family release balloons. He assumed the baby Laila was holding was Cymone's. He wanted to make himself known, but quickly decided against it. He would catch Cymone on another day. Going to the counselor and pretending to be remorseful about what he did helped him to get released early. He had written a letter to Cymone apologizing, but that was to show his counselor that he really wanted to make a change.

He had written her letters and called her, and she acted like she was too damn good to respond. Well, he would just have to show her that there was no leaving him. He had tried to warn her that if he couldn't have her nobody else would. He would rather see her dead than in the arms of another man. Maurice had seen all he wanted to see, so he drove off.

After everybody left, Steve and Laila sat in the living room and talked like old times. Cymone couldn't remember the last time she had seen her parents actually talking and smiling with each other. When she passed by, Laila motioned for her to come to her. "Come sit and talk with us for a little while. Was that the UPS guy that was here earlier?"

Cymone frowned. "Yeah, that was him."

Laila smiled. "He's cute Cymone. I can see why you didn't hesitate to give him your number."

"Ma, I hate I ever met him," Cymone replied, with a hint of disappointment in her voice.

Steve interjected. "Damn. What did he do already?"

"First of all, he used to go with Tasha, and when I introduced him to Tasha and Christi, he acted like he didn't know who she was. Tasha ran out the house crying, so Christi and I went behind her. Seems like her and Todd go way back. She met him in South Carolina when she went to visit her family. Remember after Josh funeral she was supposed to come over and didn't? Well, she was with him. I thought maybe she had slept with Josh because she started acting strange after his funeral. I'm glad to know that wasn't the case, but Mr. Todd is living foul."

"What did he do?" Laila asked.

With tears in her eyes, Cymone looked at Laila. "Ma, Todd has HIV."

Laila screamed. "What?"

Cymone sniffed. "He infected Tasha, and Nick's little sister, Teresa."

"Those poor girls. That's why I stress to you the importance of protection. Don't always rely on the man to have condoms, always carry some yourself. That way you never have to worry about him saying, 'I don't have protection. I'm clean baby. I promise I'll pull out. Did you..."

Before Laila could get the question out, Cymone stopped her. "Don't worry Ma, I never slept with him. All I did was kiss him."

Steve shook his head. "That don't make any sense. He must don't know he can go to jail for attempted murder?"

Cymone was still in disbelief herself. "He's in denial. When I confronted him about it, he said Tasha got it from somebody else because he was clean. When Nick came by and found out who he was and called him out for giving it to his little sister, he left. I guess it's just not meant for me to find love again."

"Baby girl, the right man will come along for you when it's time."

"Then on top of all of this drama Nick said Maurice is supposed to be getting out before the month is out."

"Who is Maurice?" Steve asked.

"Maurice is the young man that almost took our daughter away from us," Laila gritted her teeth at the thought of him.

"Why is he getting out?"

"Daddy, I don't know. They gave him eight years, and he's only done two. Nick said something about him seeing a counselor while he was locked up."

"More than likely he conned his counselor into believing he was remorseful and they made recommendations for him to be released early," Steve added. "Cymone don't worry about him, your daddy is back home now."

Cymone looked at her mom, then her dad in surprise.

Steve chuckled. "No not home like that, but back in your life. If I had of been around none of that would have happened. You wouldn't have had to go through that. Daddy's are supposed to protect their little girls, and I failed you terribly."

Cymone sat beside her father. "It's not your fault Daddy. I chose to be with Maurice. I could have left him the first time he hit me, but I stayed. Even after he almost beat me to death, I was debating on going back to him. I probably would have, well, I know I would have if I hadn't of caught him with Gina."

Laila spoke up. "That's not important now. You woke up and realized he wasn't the one for you."

"Ma, Daddy, it's getting late I'm gonna call it a night. JJ has left me again tonight. I swear all I did was give birth to him." Cymone kissed her parents before heading to her room. Before she walked out of the living room, she turned around and looked at her daddy. "It's good having you here Daddy. I just hope you were for real about what you said."

When Cymone opened her bedroom door, she heard her cell phone ringing. She picked the phone up off her bed and looked at the caller ID. She noticed it was Tasha calling and hurried to pick it up. "Hey girl. Everything okay?"

Tasha sighed. "Yeah, I just wanted to tell you how sorry I am."

"What do you have to be sorry for Tasha?"

"Christi told me that you were really feeling some guy you met that drives for UPS. She said you sounded happy when you talked about him. I know you haven't dated or wanted to date since Josh died. Then when you meet somebody you're interested in, this shit happens."

[218]

"Tash, it's not your fault."

"Mone, if I had of told you and Christi about him when I first met him, none of this would have happened."

"You are not to blame Tasha, so leave it alone."

"Did you like him?" Tasha asked.

"Everything was perfect with him. Too perfect if you ask me. We had a lot of things in common, and it was easy to talk to him. I told him about JJ and my past and he was still interested. If you hadn't of told me what he did to you, I probably would have slept with him. There's no need to apologize or feel guilty. I need to be thanking you for saving my life. Why didn't you tell us when you first found out? We could have been there for you."

"I don't know. I thought things would be different between us. I felt that y'all wouldn't want to be around me anymore."

"Tasha you are my friend. I consider you my sister. There's no way I would have ever turned my back on you and if you're trying to compare this situation to what me and Chris went through, you can't. They're two totally different situations. I'm here for you whenever you need me."

"Thanks, Mone that really means a lot. You just don't know how hard it's been. Christi came over after I kept ignoring her calls. She made me get up off my ass and do something with myself. I just wanted to sit in this house and die, but knowing my girls are still here for me makes living worthwhile."

"I'm glad you realize that," Cymone said.

"Mone it's late, and I know it's been past your bedtime I'll talk you with you tomorrow. Goodnight." Tasha was beyond grateful to have such honest, loving friends.

"Goodnight girl, see you tomorrow."

Chapter 19

Nick heard a knock at the door, he looked out the peephole and got the shock of his life. "What the fuck?" Nick said opening the door.

There stood Maurice with a big ass smirk on his face. He could see the shocked expression on Nick's face. "Surprise to see me?" Maurice asked. Nick was so shocked he could hardly get his words out. "You said before the end of the month is out, so I was looking for you at the end of the month, not now."

"Damn, nigga. You ain't gone invite me in?"

Nick smiled nervously. "Oh, my bad, come in. How long you been out?"

"I've been home a few days now. I just been laying low. You know trying to make this shit work with Gina." Maurice made his way in the door, looking around.

"That's what's up. What brings you by here?"

"Damn, I'm offended. You my homeboy and I ain't seen you in two years. I just wanted to come by and see how you doing."

"Maurice, let's cut out all the bullshit. I've known you too long. You called and threatened me. You called to let me know you were getting out. Now you just pop up at my spot. What's up?"

"Have you seen Cymone?" Maurice asked glaring at Nick.

"I went by her house on the 4th of July and told her you were getting out sometime this month."

"How did she take the news?" Maurice questioned.

"I mean she said she was happy for you and she wished the best for you and Gina." Nick replied nonchalantly.

"You told her me and Gina were back together?" Maurice asked frowning.

Nick looked confused. "Why, I wasn't supposed to tell her?"

"Nawl, it ain't that. I just wanted to be the one to tell her."

"You planning on contacting her?"

"Eventually, we'll run into each other. Then I can finish what I started."

"Dude, you got to be kidding me. You just got out and you trying to go back."

"Nick, I ain't going back to prison. I did two years in that hell hole, ain't no going back for me. Your conscience still bugging you?" Maurice asked.

"What you mean by that?" Nick glared at his former friend, tired of his games.

"You acted like you felt bad about killing that punk ass nigga Mone was with. I thought you would have confessed by now." Maurice laughed.

"It bothers me to know that I'm the one that caused Mone all the pain I see in her eyes. I want to tell her everything about the situation, but I'm not trying to go to jail. She already suspects you. She just don't have any proof."

Maurice walked up to Nick and stabbed him in the chest so quick, Nick never saw it coming. Maurice pulled

[222]

back and drove the knife into Nick's chest one last time and then slowly, soflty whispered into his ear. "And she never will." Then he stood there, watching his old friend bleed to death.

Nick lay there gasping for air. He closed his eyes and asked God to forgive him for taking Josh's life. He prayed, asking God to take him quick and not let him suffer. He also prayed the letter he wrote Mone confessing everything reached her. Nick knew Maurice would come for him once he was released from prison. That's why after he left Cymone's house on the 4th of July he wrote her a letter explaining what he did to Josh and why. He had a nagging feeling all day; he just couldn't put his finger on what was bugging him. So he mailed the letter to Cymone earlier that day.

Nick died a peaceful death knowing that his friend would soon meet his own fate. Maurice smiled wickedly as Nick took his last breath. Maurice left Nick's house feeling elated. He knew his secret had just died with Nick, or so he thought. Maurice would soon find out that karma is truly a bitch.

****

Laila walked in the house and placed the mail on the kitchen table. When Cymone heard her Mom come in, she ran into the kitchen where she was. "Hey, ma. Did I get any mail?"

Laila pointed at the stack of mail on the kitchen table. "That's what I got out the box. I haven't had a chance to go through it." Getting the bottle of wine out the refrigerator, Laila sat to the table. "Did Martha say when she's bringing JJ home?" She got comfortable, pouring a glass of wine.

"Nawl, she act like she's the only person who can spend time with him'. Cymone said picking up the mail and going through it. It was mainly junk mail and bills. Cymone came across an envelope addressed to her with no return address and put it to the side.

Laila chuckled. She too felt the same way. Ever since JJ had been in the world Martha has been the one who has kept him majority of the time. Laila nor Cymone complained because they knew she missed Josh. JJ was the spitting image of his dad and they knew that's why Martha wanted to keep him so much. JJ was a very smart little boy and he knew Cymone was mommy.

"You want a home cooked meal or do you wanna do take out?" Laila asked.

"Can we order Pizza and Wings from Papa John's?"

Laila smiled. "That's fine with me."

[224]

"Did I have any important mail besides bills?" Laila asked sipping on her wine.

"No Ma, that's all that really came. I got a letter, but it has no name or return address on it."

"What kind of pizza you want?"

"Pepperoni and supreme."

Laila picked up the phone, called Papa John's and ordered the pizza. Before she could return the cordless phone to the base, it began ringing. Laila answered on the second ring. "Hello, I'm good. How you doing? Yes, she's here hold on." Laila held the phone out for Cymone. "It's Christi." She whispered.

Cymone grabbed the phone from her mother. "Hey Chris. What's up? No, I haven't watched the news today. What happened? What? No! What happened to him? Oh my God. He was just over here on the 4th of July. No, I hadn't talked to him since. He looked like he wanted to say something to me, but he never did. The only thing he told me was that Maurice was supposed to be getting out this month. He said he didn't want me to run into him and be surprised. Ok, thanks for calling me." Cymone hung up the phone in disbelief, and it showed all over her face.

"Baby girl, what's wrong?"

"Christi said she saw on the news that Nick was found stabbed to death in his house."

Laila covered her mouth in shock. "Do they know who did it? He seemed like a nice young man. Who would want to hurt him?"

"I don't know, ma. This seems so unreal. I mean it was just last week he was here. Who would want him dead?"

Laila walked over to her daughter and rubbed her back. "Mone are you gonna be okay?"

"Yes, ma. It's just shocking."

"That goes to show you that tomorrow is not promised to any of us. One day we're here the next we're not." Laila reminded her daughter.

****

Nick was laid to rest one week after he was found dead in his house. The church was packed. He had just as many people at his funeral as Josh did. Everyone spoke highly about him. When his sister stood up and told stories about how it was growing up with him people stopped crying and started laughing. Teresa went on to say there was no reason to be sad because Nick was no longer here. She felt everybody should rejoice because he no longer had to live in this cruel world.

[226]

After the funeral, everybody went to the cemetery to say their final goodbye to Nick. Cymone turned around to leave and walked right into Maurice. Her heart felt like it was about to beat out of her chest it was beating so hard.

Maurice smiled. "Hey, Mone. How you been?"

Cymone gathered her composure. "I've been good. How about you?"

Maurice rubbed his hands together. "I'm a free man, so I'm good."

Tasha and Christi walked up and asked Mone if she was ready. They didn't pay attention to the guy that was standing there talking to Mone until Maurice started talking again.

"Hey Christi. What's up Tasha?"

Christi looked at Maurice, and if looks could kill, they would be putting him in the ground right beside Nick. Christi didn't say anything, she just walked off. Tasha followed behind her, leaving Cymone standing there with Maurice.

Mone looked at her girls. "Maurice, it's nice to know you're free. I wish you well, but I have to go." Mone walked off before Maurice could respond to her.

Maurice turned and watched the girls leave. He had plans for Christi and Mone. They both would soon meet their fate, Maurice thought. He walked over to the place where Nick would be resting for eternity. He simply said, "Only if you hadn't of been so weak you would still be here now." Maurice picked up a flower and threw it on top of the casket before walking away.

Maurice drove past Cymone's house to see if she had made it home, but he didn't see any cars in the driveway. He was about to go to Christi's house until he spotted Cymone's car coming up the street. He pulled over and parked on the opposite side of the street and watched Cymone, Christi and Tasha get out of the car and walk inside the house. They were so deep in conversation they didn't notice the car parked across the street. Maurice sat there for about forty-five minutes before pulling off. As he was driving by Cymone's house, Christi was walking out of the door. She looked up and locked eyes with Maurice. He smiled and blew her a kiss. She responded by sticking her middle finger up at him.

Tasha saw what Christi did. "Who you shooting birds at?"

'That was Maurice riding by. I swear that dude is mental. I'm still trying to figure out how his crazy ass got out of prison so soon."

Cymone came out the house and noticed Christi's mood had changed. She locked the door and turned to her friend. "What's wrong Chris?"

"Mone, you may want to get a restraining order against Maurice."

"Why?"

"I think he's stalking you."

"That day Nick came over, he told me he was getting out sooner than what we thought, so I prepared myself for this. Besides Nick said he was back with Gina, so I don't think I need to worry much about him."

"Look Mone, Maurice is a straight up mental case, and I don't trust him. For your own safety get the damn restraining order against him."

Tasha added her two cents. "Mone I think Christi is right. You have to protect yourself and if getting a restraining order against that psycho will one day save your life, then you need to do it. You already know what he's capable of."

"If you don't do it for yourself do it for JJ. If Maurice had Josh killed and wanted to kill you, what makes you think he won't try to hurt JJ?" Christi stated.

Not wanting to put her son in danger, Cymone had heard enough. "Okay. Okay. Okay. I'll go down to the police department and see about getting a restraining order against him." Cymone didn't want to believe Maurice would hurt her son but giving his history she wasn't taking any chances.

****

While pulling in her driveway, Cymone thought about what Christi said about Maurice. She knew he was a jealous person, but he had no reason to be jealous over her. They were no longer together and the entire time he was locked up, she didn't give him any reason to think they would be together. She decided to go through the letters he had written her to see where his head was at. When she walked in the house, she was greeted by her parents sitting in the living room engaged in a kiss. When they heard the door close, they both jumped. Cymone didn't know what to say. She just stood there looking from her mom to her dad. Her parents thought she was waiting for an explanation.

Laila cleared her throat. "Baby girl. We can explain."

Cymone responded in a very dry tone, irritated. "Ma, you don't have to explain. You two are adults. What you two decide to do with each other is none of my business. I'm going to my room and pretend I didn't just see what I saw." Cymone went to her bedroom and pulled the letters out of her drawer. The first letter she opened Maurice was apologizing for what he had done to her. He asked for her forgiveness and told her he understood it would take time. She put the letter back in the envelope and picked up another one. This was the letter with no name or return address. She looked at all of the other letters from Maurice and noticed they all had his name and the address of the prison on it. She tore the envelope open and started reading the letter.

Dear Cymone,

I've gone over this, over and over in my head, and I know this is the right thing to do. I am so sorry for all the pain I've caused you. I know you're probably saying to yourself, "What pain?" I'm gonna just get straight to it. Maurice and I have been boys a long time. There's nothing I wouldn't do for him. Maybe one day I'll explain that to you. When Maurice asked me to do one favor for him, I agreed with no hesitation. When I found out what he wanted me to do, I knew it was wrong, but I did it anyway. I can no longer walk around carrying this guilt. When I look into your eyes and see all the pain you have inside, it breaks me down because I know I'm the one that caused you that pain. Seeing your son grow up without his father breaks my heart. Cymone, I was the one who killed Josh.

Cymone gasped and fell back on her pillows. What was he saying? Who was saying this? She continued to read feverishly, unable to take in the words fast enough.

Maurice asked me to take him out, hoping that would make you go back to him. He felt like without Josh around he would have a better chance getting you back. I am so sorry for this. I know you're going straight to the police, and it's okay. I'm ready to take my punishment.

Cymone let out a loud piercing cry. Laila and Steve ran to her bedroom to see what was going on. When they walked in her room, they found her crying and screaming hysterically.

A frantic Laila screamed, "What's wrong Mone?"

Cymone was crying so hard she couldn't say anything. Steve rubbed her back gently. "Calm down baby girl and tell us what's wrong."

Cymone pointed at the letter on the bed. Steve picked it up and started reading it. He looked at Laila with confused eyes and handed her the letter. When she read the letter, she understood why Cymone was so distraught.

"Oh my God, Mone. I'm so sorry. We need to call the police."

Barely able to speak Cymone replied. "What for ma? Nick is dead. There's nothing that can be done now."

"That's true. What about that Maurice dude? He can go back to prison if he had something to do with that boy murder," Steve admitted.

"Daddy, I don't know. Maurice was probably still locked up when Nick was killed."

"We can find that out. Where's your laptop?"

Cymone grabbed her laptop off the dresser and handed it to her dad. Steve went to the Georgia Department of Corrections website and put Maurice's information in. Looking at the computer screen Steve said. "It looks like Maurice was released on July 2nd."

Laila wiped the tears from Cymone's eyes. "Baby girl he was definitely out when Nick was killed. He probably thought by killing Nick nobody would ever find out he had something to do with Josh's murder. He couldn't have known that Nick had written you a letter confessing what happened."

"Ma, Christi told me I need to get a restraining order against him."

"I think that's a good idea. First thing in the morning, we're gonna go take care of that. I don't trust him, and I hate to have to introduce him to my "little friend."

"Laila you still got that lil pea shooter?" Steve turned towards her, amused.

Laila smiled. "No dear, I've upgraded from that lil pea shooter you bought me all those years ago."

"Mone, baby, are you gonna be okay?"

Mone wiped her nose with the tissue Steve passed to her. "Yes ma, I'll be okay."

Laila and Steve took turns hugging and kissing their daughter. "Try to get some sleep baby girl and we'll go to the police station in the morning."

"Daddy are you staying here tonight?" Steve looked at Laila like, how do I answer this?

Laila smiled. "If you want to sleep on the sofa that's fine with me."

Cymone shook her head. "Yeah right ma, don't front. Y'all were on the verge of having sex on the sofa when I walked in so I know he's not gonna be sleeping on the sofa if he stays overnight."

When Steve and Laila walked out of Cymone's room, she picked up the phone and called Christi. Christi answered on the third ring. "Did I wake you?"

[234]

"No, I'm up watching TV. What's going on? You sound like you been crying."

"Christi, I found out today that Nick killed Josh."

"WHAT? Who told you that?"

"Nick told me himself. I got a letter a few weeks ago, and I didn't open it because I thought it was from Maurice. Well, I went through the letters a little while ago and found out the letter I thought was from Maurice was really from Nick. He confessed he was the one that killed Josh."

"I don't understand. Why would Nick kill Josh?"

"Because Maurice asked him to."

"Get out of here. I can't believe this shit. He was all in your face smiling and all along he was the one that took Josh away from you and JJ. That's some foul shit Mone."

"I know when he came over on the 4th of July, he looked like he wanted to tell me something. He kept looking at me strangely."

"That guilt was eating his ass up."

"Maybe so, reading the letter he wrote I feel he was sincere when he said he was sorry for the pain he caused me. My parents are taking me to the police station in the morning to take the letter and get a restraining order against Maurice."

"That's the best thing to do because ain't no telling what be going through his sick mind."

"Yeah, but they might not do anything to him because he was in jail when Josh was killed."

"You never know Mone, they might be able to do something to him."

"Chris, I just wanted to call you and tell you that. I'm gonna try to get some sleep. I'll come by tomorrow after we leave the station."

Chapter 20

The next morning Laila and Steve took Cymone to the police station. Detective Alvarez was the lead detective on Josh's case, but he wasn't in the office yet. The nice lady at the desk told Cymone she could wait on Detective Alvarez, or she could speak with someone else. Cymone told the lady she would just wait on Detective Alvarez.

They sat in the lobby and waited three hours for him to come into the office. When he finally arrived the lady at the desk pointed at Cymone and her parents and told him they had been waiting to talk to him. She told him it was some information concerning Josh Hayes' case. Detective Alvarez thanked the lady and walked over to Cymone and her parents. Detective Alvarez held his hand out to Cymone. "Hello Ma'am. I'm Detective Alvarez."

Cymone stood up and shook the detective's hand. "I'm Cymone." Pointing at her parents, Cymone quickly introduced them. "These are my parents, Laila and Steve."

Detective Alvarez shook Laila and Steve hand as well. "Nice to meet you all. I hear you have some information for me. Why don't you all come and have a seat in my office?" They followed the detective to a nice office with lots of awards and pictures hanging on the wall.

Once they were inside, Detective Alvarez motioned for them to have a seat. "I hear you have some information regarding the Josh Hayes' case. May I ask your relation to Mr. Hayes?"

"He was my boyfriend," Cymone replied.

"Oh, I'm sorry for your loss ma'am."

Cymone handed the letter that Nick wrote to the detective. "I received that letter a few weeks ago, but I just opened it last night. I thought it was from my ex-boyfriend, so I just stuck it with the rest of his mail. Last night I decided to go through them, but I noticed all the letters from my ex had his name with a return address."

The detective took the letter out the envelope and began reading. "Who is this Nick guy?"

"Nick, he was Maurice's best friend. Nick was recently found dead in his home."

Detective Alvarez looked up from the letter. "Who is this Maurice guy?"

"He's my ex-boyfriend. He just got out of prison on two aggravated assault charges."

"We also want to see what we need to do to take out a restraining order against Maurice," Laila interrupted.

Detective Alvarez placed the letter on his desk. "Ma'am why do you need a restraining order?"

"Maurice went to prison for pulling a gun out on my daughter. Several months later her boyfriend was killed. Before all of that happened, Maurice beat my daughter within an inch of her life. He's always saying if he can't have her no one else will. We don't want to take any chances with her safety," Laila replied.

"Was there a police report or charges filed against him for that?"

Cymone cleared her throat. "No sir, I didn't press charges. I told the officers that questioned me I didn't know who had beat me." She said lowering her head in shame.

"I see. Ma'am in cases such as domestic violence it's very important to always file charges. That way there's a record of the abuse. Ms. Cymone, do you feel you're in danger?"

Cymone looked at her parents then at the detective. "Yes, I do. The entire time he was locked up he called and wrote me. I never wrote him back, but I ended up answering one of his calls. I felt like if I answered and gave him a chance to say what he wanted to say he would stop calling me. He acted like he's sorry, and he's been begging me to forgive him, but I've heard it all before. That night when he pulled the gun on me and told me that if he couldn't have me no one else would, I truly believed he was gonna kill me. He would have succeeded if it wasn't for the officer that pulled up and seen him pointing the gun at me. The hate I seen in his eyes was real. I didn't see anything that would suggest he had ever loved me. What's so frustrating about the whole thing is, I don't know why he feels that way about me? I never cheated on him. The only thing I did was leave him. It's not just me anymore; I have a son to think about now."

Detective Alvarez held the letter up. "I'm gonna look into these allegations, but in the meantime let's get this restraining order started. Once he's been served papers he may call you, if he does, call us. The restraining order will advise him that he can't be within 50 feet of you or your house. He will not be permitted to contact you via phone, text or email. If he does either, you call us. If he does any of those things he'll be in direct violation of the order and he will be arrested. Domestic violence restraining orders usually last a year, but I'm gonna request two years on this one. Just remember in two years come and go through this all over again."

Cymone looked at Detective Alvarez with so much compassion. "Thank you. Thank you so much."

"Does she need to go before the judge?" Steve inquired.

"All she has to do is sign the papers. I'll give them to the judge to sign off on, and once the judge's signature is on them, I'll personally deliver them to Mr. Smith. You will get a copy of the order in the mail in a few days. Make sure you put it up in a safe place. If you ever have to call the police about him, you'll need to show them the order."

Steve, Laila and Cymone thanked the detective again and walked out of his office feeling like the weight of the world had been lifted off of them.

Steve and Laila dropped Cymone off at Christi's house. Cymone told Christi everything the detective said.

"Do you think he's gonna follow the order?" Christi asked.

"I don't know, I hope he does. I don't have any ill feelings toward him. I forgave him a long time ago for what he did to me, not for him, but for myself. After I got out of the hospital and caught him with Gina that shit broke my heart. After all the shit he had done to me, I still loved him and wanted to be with him. Here I am, with permanent scars and a permanent limp because of him. I just found out he had the one man that truly loved me and the father of my son killed and I still don't wish him harm." Cymone shook her head.

"Mone, girl you are better than me. He raped me and got me pregnant and to this day I pray he would just fall dead. I know it's wrong, but what he did to me is unforgivable."

"Where Ms. Pat? I haven't seen her since the 4th of July."

"Girl, I didn't tell you, she's on vacation. Her ass went to Miami."

"Miami? Lord, don't tell me she in Florida with Uncle Mike."

Christi started laughing "Okay, I won't tell you then."

Cymone shook her head smirking at the thought of Ms. Pat and her Uncle Mike together.

"I take it JJ is with Mrs. Martha." Christi said.

"You already know it. I appreciate everything she's done since he's been in this world but I miss my baby. Every time I call her to see when she's bringing him home, she tells me I'll bring him tomorrow."

"Let me guess, tomorrow never comes." Christi said laughing.

Cymone chuckled. "Hell nawl, I try to be understanding and let her spend as much time with him as possible because I know she misses Josh but I loved him too and having my son with me is like having a piece of him back." Cymone sadly said.

"Maybe you should sit her down and explain that to her." Christi offered.

"Yea, you right." Cymone replied. Just then there was a knock at the door. "Christi you expecting company?" Cymone said looking towards the door.

"It might be Tasha. She said she was gonna come by after she left the doctor." Christi said walking to the door. Assuming it was Tasha at the door she didn't look to see who was knocking she just opened the door. Christi got the shock of her life when she looked into the eyes of Maurice and not Tasha. She gawked at him. "What the fuck you want Maurice?" Christi spoke in a harsh tone.

"Is Cymone here?" Maurice asked dismissing Christi's attitude.

Christi tried to slam the door, but Maurice stuck his foot in the way to prevent it from closing.

"I asked you a question. Is Cymone here?" He barked angrily.

Cymone heard Maurice at the door and to keep confusion down she walked to the door. "What do you want Maurice?"

[243]

"Mone you know what I want. Why the fuck you take out a restraining order against me?"

"Oh, so you got served already? Damn, Detective Alvarez moved fast." Cymone said sarcastically.

"So, you think this shit funny Mone?" Maurice boomed, glaring at Cymone with those menacing eyes.

"No, you're funny. Why are you here Maurice? How did you even know I was here? Shouldn't you be home with Gina?" Cymone said with her arms folded across her chest.

"I'm about to call the police because you are clearly violating your order by being here." Christi said walking towards the phone.

"Bitch, you touch that phone, and I'll blow your fucking brains out. Now try me." Maurice said pointing a gun at Christi.

Christi turned around and saw the 9mm Maurice held in his hand. She stood frozen in fear. Christi was so petrified she almost urinated on herself.

Maurice walked inside the house, closed and locked the door. He pointed the gun at Cymone and motioned for her to go sit down.

"Maurice, why are you here? I mean why can't you just leave me alone?" Cymone asked with tears in her eyes.

Maurice walked up to her and wiped the tears from her eyes before they fell. "Mone, don't you see how much I love you. I told you nobody else would have you and as you can see I meant that. I would rather see you dead than to walk the streets every day and not be able to have you." Maurice turned his attention to Christi. "Don't look at me like that. You need to be praying for your own life. I ain't forgot that foul shit you did to me."

Christi couldn't believe her ears, and she snapped. "Foul. Nigga, you calling me foul?" Nigga you raped me." Christi screamed.

"I didn't rape you, but that's what you wanted Cymone to believe." Maurice spat on her.

"You got me pregnant and lied to Cymone about it." Christi wasn't going to be silenced. "You tried to come between me and my friend and it almost worked, but as you can see we're better than ever."

"Bitch I should just kill you now, like you killed my baby."

In a calm, but stern voice Christi said, "You do what you have to do Maurice. I'm not afraid to die. If I wanted to kill my baby, I would have just had an abortion. I miscarried him. God knew how he was conceived. He knew what kind of person you were. I didn't want to bring

[245]

a baby into this world having you as a father, but I couldn't just kill him. God heard my heart and took him from me, so if you want to kill me go right ahead." Christi said spreading her arms out.

"Maurice put the gun down. You don't need it. If you want me to leave with you, I will. Just put the gun away. Chris has nothing to do with this. You can't be mad at her for having a miscarriage. If you hadn't of been a grimy ass nigga and raped her, none of that would have happened. Did you ever stop to think about how she may have felt about the situation? She's the one that carried the baby and bonded with him."

"Mone, I see you've grown a backbone since I've been locked up. When we were together you never tried to talk to me like this. Is it because you have a baby now?"

"Well Maurice, a lot of shit done changed. You came up in here waving a gun at us talking shit acting like a fucking mad man and for what? You killed my boyfriend. You had the one man that truly loved me killed. Hell, you probably had Nick killed or did you do that yourself? I don't even know who you are anymore. What happened to the guy I met in footlocker all those years ago?" Cymone said, purposely not answering his question about her son.

While Cymone was talking to Maurice, Christi had managed to get her cell phone without Maurice seeing her. She texted Tasha and told her to call the police and have them come to her house pronto. She knew Tasha wouldn't ask any questions, she would just call them. Christi just prayed Maurice was bluffing with the gun.

Maurice grabbed Mone by the face and looked deep into her eyes. "I loved you. I still love you. That Josh dude couldn't and wouldn't love you the way I do."

Cymone snatched her face out of his hands. "You right Maurice nobody has loved me the way you did. If that was love you showed me. I never want to be loved again. Answer me this. How did you get Nick to kill Josh?"

Maurice smirked. "All I did was ask."

"Don't anybody risk their freedom just because a friend asks them to do something."

"Nick and I been cool for a long time. Nick's stepfather was a pervert. His mom worked the night shift, and his stepdad was home with him. Well, the dad had a secret he kept from Nick's mom. He didn't let her know that he liked fucking little boys in the ass. Nick's mom let Teresa stay with her grandmother because she didn't feel comfortable leaving her with the stepdad not knowing even if she had left her he wouldn't have touched her. Teresa didn't have what he wanted. Nick broke down one day and told me what was going on, and that shit disgusted me so bad. I mean, why would a grown man, a grown married man, want to have sex with a little boy?"

Maurice paced the room, waving the gun around nonchalantly. "When Nick asked me if I could help him, I told him I would take care of it for him. I was at Nick's house one night, and his stepdad had been drinking. He must have thought I had left because he cornered Nick and told him it was time to take care of daddy. He wanted Nick to suck his dick before he fucked him. Seeing this man try to take advantage of my friend sickened me. Nick's stepdad was about 6'3", 350lbs and Nick, well you know how little he was as an adult. Just imagine how small he was when he was a kid. He dropped his pants and his boxers and made Nick get down on his knees in front of him. Nick kept saying he didn't want to do it, but the sick bastard just laughed. He had his back turned to me, so I snuck up behind him and hit him over the head with Nick's baseball bat. He grabbed his head and turned around.

"When he saw me, he lunged at me. I guess he forgot his pants were around his ankles. He ended up falling flat on his face. I didn't even see Nick leave the living room. The next thing I knew Nick was on top of the old man stabbing him like his life depended on it. I still had the bat in my hands, so while Nick was stabbing him, I was beating him. I grabbed the knife from Nick, cut his dick off and shoved it in his mouth. We cleaned up and went to my house until his mom got off work. I promised him I would never say anything about it. He told me he owed me his life, that if I needed anything regardless what it was he would do it, no questions asked. When I asked him to take Josh out he didn't hesitate."

"If you and Nick were friends like that, and you went through all of that to protect him, why did you kill him?"

Before Maurice could answer there was a loud knock at the door. "Police, open up."

Maurice looked at Christi angrily. "You bitch." He pointed the gun at her and pulled the trigger but nothing happened. The damn thing jammed. Maurice knew he had nowhere to run, so he dropped the gun, got down on his knees and placed his hands behind his head. He told Cymone. "Go ahead and let them in."

Cymone walked over to the door and opened it.

The officer asked, "Ma'am are you okay? We got a call from Tasha saying to come here, but she didn't know what was wrong."

"Officer everything is okay." Cymone said somberly.

Christi ran to the door. "No, everything is not okay officer." Pointing at Maurice dramatically, she said. "He is not supposed to be within 50 feet of my friend. He came over here and pulled a gun out on us and threatened to kill me. When you knocked on the door, he pointed the gun at me and pulled the trigger. By the grace of God the damn thing jammed, I want to press charges."

The officer looked at Cymone. "Ma'am is this true? Do you have a restraining order against this gentleman?"

"Yes I do, but I haven't received a copy of the order. I just took the order out this morning."

The officer walked in the house and saw Maurice on the floor. He walked over to him and motioned for him to stand up. The officer proceeded to read Maurice his Miranda rights while handcuffing him.

The officer escorted Maurice outside, but not before Christi spat in his face. "I hope you rot in jail you sick son of a bitch."

Maurice smirked wickedly. "They can't hold me forever." He pursed his lips and kissed at Christi. "I'll see you again real soon."

The officer looked at Christi. "Ma'am you're gonna have to come to the station and give a written statement." He then looked at Cymone. "Ma'am, you'll need to write one as well."

Chapter 21

Christi and Cymone went to the police station and gave their written statements. Cymone had mixed feelings about Maurice after hearing what he did for Nick. Christi's phone kept vibrating while she was writing her statement. She knew it was Tasha calling so she shot her a quick text and told her she would call her when she got home.

When the girls left the police station, Cymone asked Christi if she would drop her off at home. Christi dropped Mone off and headed home. As soon as she walked in her house she called Tasha.

"Damn, you just getting home?"

"Yeah, I had to drop Mone off at home."

"What happened? Why did you want me to call and have the police come to your house?"

"Girl, Maurice came over here looking for Mone. This nigga pulled a gun out on us. He pointed the gun at me and pulled the trigger, but thank God the damn thing jammed."

"OMG! Are you okay? What about Mone? Is she okay?" Tasha got it all out in one breath.

"Yeah, I'm okay. I'm just pissed. Mone is okay, but she acted like she didn't want to write the statement. She had gone to the police station earlier and took out a restraining order against Maurice. She also gave the police a letter Nick wrote her telling her that Maurice asked him to kill Josh."

"WHAT? Are you saying Nick killed Josh?" This was too much. Tasha tried to take it all in.

"Yep, that's what it looks like."

"Why wouldn't Mone want to write a statement? That was her boyfriend and the father of her baby."

"I don't know. He told her some story about how he saved Nick from his abusive stepfather."

Tasha popped her lips. "She better not fall for that shit."

"Tasha, I believe she already has. If you could have seen the look on her face."

"What did they do to Maurice?"

"They locked him up for violating his restraining order."

"What about him pointing the gun at you?"

"It's my word against theirs. Mone said he didn't, he said he didn't, and I said he did."

"You kidding me right?" Tasha said not believing her ears.

"I wish I was. I wanted to slap some sense into her. All this time she's been saying she's through with him now it's a whole different story. I wouldn't be surprised if she doesn't take him back."

"Even after finding out he had Josh killed?"

"Yes. Look enough about that mess. How did your doctor appointment go?"

"It went okay. I got some more medicine. I told him I don't be having any energy, so he prescribed me some iron pills."

"I'm glad you're okay."

Tasha knew Christi loved Mone like a sister. She could hear the hurt in her voice. "Christi don't worry so much about Mone. She knows Maurice is bad news."

"I hope you're right Tasha. I really hope you're right."

****

When Cymone got home she went straight to her bedroom. So much had happened she just needed to be alone and become one with her thoughts. She couldn't understand why she was feeling so much sympathy for Maurice. He had beat her, killed her boyfriend, pulled a gun out on her not once, but twice and here she was having mixed feelings about him. She knew right then despite everything he had done she still loved him.

Cymone lay on her bed holding her brown bear with the red heart in the middle of his stomach and thought about happier times with Maurice. Things hadn't always been bad between them. Her mom nor her friends ever got a chance to see the kinder side of him. Yes, he got her best friend pregnant, but that was just as much Christi's fault as it was his. She had forgiven her and rekindled their friendship, so why couldn't she rekindle her relationship with Maurice. She knew her parents, Christi, and Tasha would be mad if she got back with Maurice, but who cares what they think, I have to do what's best for me and my son. Just then her cell phone rang. "Hello."

"Hey, Mone. What are you doing?"

"Nothing, I was just laying here thinking about you."

"Oh yeah, I hope all good thoughts."

Cymone smiled. "They actually were good thoughts. Have you found out what they gonna do to you?"

"I may have to do some time, no more than two years. Are you gonna be waiting for me when I come home?"

"I can't promise you that Maurice. I was laying here thinking about how things use to be between us. I feel like a complete fool right now for even considering being with you again." "You shouldn't feel like that Mone, the heart can't help what the heart wants."

"You right. Why does my heart want a man who has caused me enough pain to last three lifetimes?"

"Mone I can be better. I will be better for you. Just give me a chance to show you.

"What about Gina?" Cymone questioned.

"What about Gina?" Maurice snapped.

"Aren't you and her back together?"

"Look Mone Gina is cool. She held me down while I was locked up. She did all the things I hoped you would do so I'll be forever grateful to her. I don't love her. I've never loved her. I love only you."

"You sure as hell had a funny way of showing it."

"Baby, that's the only way I knew how to. Talking to my counselor helped me realize what I was doing was wrong. I truly am sorry for the pain I caused you."

"I forgive you Maurice and I'm not saying I'm gonna take you back. I have son who depends on me. Let's just take it one day at a time and see where it leads.

"Wow, you finally admitted it. May I ask by who?" Maurice asked feeling like his heart had been ripped out this chest.

Cymone sighed and silently prayed she didn't make a mistake by telling Maurice she had a son. "Josh is his father." She said just above a whisper.

Maurice could feel himself about to explode so he inhaled and exhaled repeatedly until he felt calm enough to respond. "I can accept him and be that male role model in his life."

Cymone hesitated. "No disrespect Maurice but you had his father killed. I wouldn't want you to be a part of his life. I'm not sure if I want you to be a part of my life yet."

"If I have to do time, are you gonna accept my calls and respond to my letters? Maybe visit me once in a while." Maurice asked, changing the subject.

"I can do that." Cymone replied.

"Having you by my side will make the time go by fast. I'll have something to look forward to. Mone the guard was nice enough to let me use his cell phone. I don't want to wear it out in case I need to use it again. I'll call you and let you know what's going on. I love you, Mone."

"I love you too Maurice."

Maurice disconnected the call feeling like he just conquered the world.

****

Maurice ended up with two years jail time. Cymone kept the fact that she was corresponding with Maurice from her parents and friends. She had her letters sent to a PO Box so her mom wouldn't find out she was writing Maurice. They talked on the phone every night and wrote each other once a week. Maurice told her that he enjoyed hearing his name called for mail because some of the inmates never got mail. That's why even though they talked every night she still wrote him too.

Cymone still talked to Christi and Tasha just not as much. She knew they wouldn't approve of her getting back with Maurice. She knew Laila wouldn't approve either, but what could she say when she had gotten back with Steve. Cymone was now living at home with her mother and her father, but it wasn't like she thought it would be. She was happy that her mom was happy again, and it was even better because it was her father that was making her happy. After all the BS, they had been through they managed to find their way back to each other. It seemed their relationship was better than ever. They were even talking about getting remarried. That's why Cymone decided it

[258]

was best she got a place for her and JJ. She was twenty-four and still living at home with her parents. She had been working for almost a year doing Medical Billing from home. The pay was good and on top of that her parents helped her out.

Cymone went to her parents and expressed to them that she felt like it was time for her and JJ to move out. At first Laila protested but Steve understood his daughter need for her own space and privacy. He agreed to pay her security deposit and the first six months of her rent. Laila warmed up to the idea and plus she didn't want to be out did by Steve so she told Cymone she would buy her furniture and whatever else she needed for her apartment. Cymone was ecstatic. All she had to do was find an apartment, and her parents would take care of the rest. She couldn't wait to talk to Maurice and let him know she was moving out.

Two weeks later, Cymone was in her own apartment. She couldn't believe that she had her own place. She called Tasha and Christi and invited them over for girls' night. They hadn't really been together, and Cymone wanted to spend time with them before Maurice came home.

Tasha arrived first. She walked in and looked around. "Girl, this is nice. I didn't know what you wanted, so I brought Tequila for the card game and Absolute and cranberry juice for drinks. I think Christi is bringing some weed. You know how she do."

Cymone laughed. "She already told me she was bringing weed and blunts. I ordered pizza and wings, and it should be here in a little bit."

By the time they put the stuff down on the table there was a knock at the door. Cymone opened the door. "You're just in time we about to fix drinks."

Christi walked in and had the same reaction as Tasha. "I like this. Girl this is nice. Did you pick out the furniture or did Ms. Laila pick it out?"

"You already know. She told me since she was paying for it she should be able to pick what she wanted. This being my apartment didn't matter, so to keep from arguing with her I let her do what she do best... Shop!"

Looking around admiring everything Christi said. "She did a good job. Tasha, how are you feeling?"

"I feel like I need a drink."

"I feel the same way." Cymone said laughing.

"What do we have to drink ladies?"

"Tequila, Absolute and cranberry juice," Tasha answered.

"We must be playing Tonk for shots?"

"You already know," Cymone stated.

"I bought a deck of cards just for this occasion."

There was a knock at the door. Cymone walked to the door. "This must be the pizza." She opened the door, signed the receipt and grabbed the pizza boxes and wings. "Food is here ladies. Christi make sure you eat first because you already know you'll be taking the most shots."

"Ha, Ha, Ha, very funny."

"Aww... Christi don't get mad. You already know you be the one to take the most shots. I got the perfect shot glass for you." Cymone held the shot glass up for Christi to read.

"*Shut up and take your shot*. Real cute Mone." Christi said, rolling her eyes.

The girls ate their pizza before they did anything. After they were through eating Christi rolled up the weed she had. She put all three blunts in rotation. They played a few games of Tonk and just like Cymone and Tasha said, Christi took a majority of the shots. They took advantage of the fact that she wasn't that good at playing cards. Christi had no idea that Cymone and Tasha were teaming up on

[261]

her. They drank so much they all passed out on the living room floor.

Cymone forgot to charge her cell phone so when Maurice called, it went straight to voicemail. He tried to reach her for over an hour and each time it went to voicemail. He knew she had moved into her apartment, and the only thing he kept thinking was she was with another nigga ignoring his calls. He had no idea she was passed out drunk with her girls.

****

Cymone woke up and noticed Tasha and Christi had already left. They had even straightened up and took out the trash. Cymone said to herself, "How the hell I sleep through all that?" When she walked into the kitchen, she saw a note on the refrigerator.

"Mone, you were sleeping so peacefully we didn't want to wake you. We cleaned up the mess and put the leftover pizza and wings in the refrigerator. Your cell was on the counter dead, so I put it in your room on the charger. We'll talk to you later, Christi."

Cymone smiled and went to her bedroom to get in the bed. As soon as her head hit the pillow, her cell phone rang. She started to ignore the call, but decided against it.

She grabbed the phone off her nightstand and answered it. As soon as she said hello Maurice went in on her.

"Where the fuck you been? Why you ain't been answering your phone? What nigga you laying up with?" He went on and on asking questions, one after another.

Cymone waited until he was through. "Are you gonna let me talk or what? I've been home all night. Christi and Tasha came over last night, and we had girl's night. We did a lot of drinking and smoking. I forgot to charge my phone so before you call here throwing accusations at me get your facts straight. I had a lot to drink last night, and I'm not feeling too good right now. I'm not in the right frame of mind to deal with this shit you dishing out. Call me later when you calm down and can talk to me like you got some fucking sense." Cymone didn't give Maurice a chance to respond before hanging up on him. She knew he would call right back, so she turned her ringer off and went back to sleep. She would deal with Maurice later.

****

Maurice couldn't believe Mone talked to him like that and hung up on him. He called her right back, and the phone just rang. He was so furious he couldn't contain his anger. He only had four more months before he was once again a free man. He knew once he touchdown he was going to have to get Cymone back in line. He wouldn't have her talking to him like he was a lame. She would definitely regret how she tried to handle him.

Chapter 22

Cymone ignored Maurice's calls for the entire week. He called every day all day and each time he called she sent him to voicemail. She had to show him that she wasn't going to tolerate the foolishness this time around. She had too much going on to deal with his insecurities. Her parents were getting married on the 4th of July, and that was only a few months away.

Just then her cell phone rang. She thought it was Maurice, but when she looked at her caller ID, she saw it was her mom. She smiled and answered. "Hey, ma."

"Hey, baby girl. Are you busy today?"

"Ma, I'm never too busy for you."

"I want to go pick out a few things for the wedding and spend some time with my favorite daughter."

"Ma, I'm your only daughter. Are you picking me up or do I need to come over there?"

"If you can come over here that would be great."

"Okay, give me an hour, I have to get dressed. Dinner on you?"

Laila sighed. "Yes, it's on me."

Cymone laughed. "I'll see you in a little bit."

An hour and thirty minutes later Cymone was in her car headed to her mom's house.

Her phone rang four times in the fifteen minutes it took to get there. When she pulled up in the driveway, she decided to answer the phone. As soon as she answered all she heard was, "Bitch who the fuck you think you playing with?"

"Look, Maurice, I don't have time for this shit. I done told you if you can't talk to me like you got some sense not to call me. I told you what happened that night. I can't make you believe me. I do know I'm having second thoughts about this whole thing. You locked up tripping on me. What's gone happen when you get home, and shit don't go your way? I can't have my son subjected to this foolishness."

"What you saying Mone?"

"I'm saying I don't think I want to get back with you."

"You think it's gone be that easy? Mone you've been my girl for years now, and now you got your own spot you want to cut me loose. What nigga been staying with you?"

"See, that's your problem. You always thinking it's another nigga. I've been enjoying my independence without a man. You haven't changed Maurice, and I'm not trying to go through the same shit with you."

"Mone you know what I told you?"

"Yeah, yeah, yeah, I know. If you can't have me nobody else will." Cymone sang.

"Are you taking me for a joke?"

"No, I'm not taking you for a joke. I'm just tired of hearing the same shit from you. You've been screaming that shit for a long time now."

"I see how it is now. Don't worry, I won't bother you ever again. After today, you won't hear from me. Enjoy your life Mone because I'm ending that shit as soon as I get home. You can take that check to the bank and cash it. I promise you it won't bounce."

"Are you through Maurice?"

"Yeah."

Before he could say anything else, Cymone disconnected the call. She had had enough of the threats. She felt foolish for thinking he had changed or could ever change. She knew he had at least another year to go so she wasn't going to sweat it.

Cymone didn't know that he would be released in June. She didn't know that was what he wanted to share with her the night he kept calling her and his calls kept

[267]

going to voicemail. Cymone would soon find out that Maurice was nothing to play with, and she should have taken his threats more seriously.

****

It was now July. The night before the wedding Cymone stayed at her Mom's house. They ordered Chinese food and watched movies. They stayed up doing each other's nails and talking. Steve decided to stay at a hotel to give the girls time alone. He didn't want to be away from them, but Laila convinced him by saying it was bad luck for them to see each other before the wedding. JJ was spending his last night with Martha. Cymone had explained to Martha that JJ needed to be home with her sometimes. Martha wasn't happy about what Cymone said but she understood where she was coming from.

"Mone, thanks for staying with me last night. I really enjoyed it, and I appreciate you for not inviting Christi and Tasha."

"You don't have to thank me. I wanted to spend time with just you. I'm so happy for you ma. Daddy has been the man he should have been all those years ago. I wish Jarvis was here to witness this special moment. Ma, I'm gonna go shower, so I won't have to rush to get dressed."

While Cymone was in the shower, there was a knock at the door. Laila didn't look to see who it was at the door, she just opened it. When she opened the door, Maurice barged in, then closed and locked it.

"What the fuck you doing here?" Laila screamed.

Maurice punched Laila in the face. "Shut the fuck up. Where's Cymone bitch?" Laila didn't respond so he punched her again. "Where's Cymone?" Laila still didn't respond. Maurice was just about to hit her again, but this time Laila was prepared. She moved out the way of the punch and landed one of her own. That shit caught Maurice off guard. Laila didn't give him time to absorb the hit before she landed another one. He grabbed Laila by her neck and started choking her. Laila tried to get his hands from around her throat, but he was just too strong. She felt herself getting weaker and weaker.

Just then she heard Cymone coming out of the bathroom. She knew if he was doing this to her, she could only imagine what he had in store for Mone. She had to save her baby. Laila gathered strength from somewhere and reached down and grabbed a hand full of Maurice nuts. She twisted and squeezed with all her might. Maurice let out a scream and let Laila go. He fell to his knees holding himself. "You bitch." He growled out in pain.

[269]

Laila had regained her composure and managed to grab the lamp off the end table and hit Maurice over the head with it. It knocked him down but didn't knock him out. She ran down the hall screaming. Cymone looked up and saw her mom running towards her with a bloody face screaming. Cymone looked confused. She didn't know what was going on.

Just then Maurice appeared. Cymone was frozen. She couldn't move or speak." Here Maurice was in her mother's house pointing a gun at her for the third time. She thought he had at least a year left, but here he was. Laila jumped in front of Mone to shield her from Maurice. Mone moved from behind Laila.

"It's okay ma." Cymone knew Maurice was never going to leave her alone. If she had to die just to be at peace, then she was ready to meet her maker. She couldn't go on living her life in fear. She knew then she couldn't be with him again. It was obvious that he really didn't love her. He just loved hurting her and the people she loved. Maurice smiled at Cymone.

"The look on your face right now is priceless. I know I'm the last person you was expecting to see."

Mone looked at Maurice with tears in her eyes. "Why Maurice? Why can't you just leave me alone? You come here on my mom's wedding day and do this shit. Look at my mom's face. You ain't have to do that shit Maurice. My mom ain't did shit to you." Maurice walked up on Mone and slapped her in the face.

"Keep your hands off my daughter." Laila yelled.

Maurice pointed the gun at Laila. "Or else what? Get your ass in the room." He pushed them both in Cymone's old room. Laila and Cymone sat down on the bed. Maurice paced back and forth scratching his head with the butt of the gun. "Cymone all you had to do was love me and be there for me, but you couldn't do that. When you got your apartment, you started acting brand new. I call you, and you would send me to voicemail."

Laila looked at Cymone surprised.

Maurice laughed. "Oh mommy dearest, you didn't know your precious little Cymone had gotten back with the big bad wolf? The first year I was back inside I talked to Mone every day, got a letter once a week and on top of that she visited me once a month. We had made plans to be together. She even told me how much she loved me."

Cymone looked at her Mom. "I'm sorry ma. Okay Maurice the cat is out the bag now. What do you want? Why are you here?"

"Mone I told you I would see you dead before I let another nigga have you. You just thought I was talking just to hear myself talk."

Cymone rubbed her earlobe. "Okay, I'll leave with you, and you can do whatever you want to me. My mom has nothing to do with this. Today is her wedding day, and my dad is waiting at the church for her. Please let her go."

Maurice smiled. "Mom and dad getting married today?" Maurice said mockingly. "I don't think dad will say I do with her face looking like that."

Laila sat there studying Maurice. He had the gun, but he didn't have a good grip on it. He was agitated and couldn't stand still. Laila didn't know if he was high on something, or he was just crazy as hell. She knew she wasn't gonna let him harm her or Cymone anymore. She had to think fast.

As soon as Maurice took his eyes off of them, Laila jumped up and punched him in the face as hard as she could. Maurice swung his hand forgetting he was holding the gun and hit Laila in the head with the butt of it. Cymone jumped on his back and clawed at his face. Blood was running down the side of Laila's head. She was momentarily dazed by the blow to her head. Maurice slung Cymone off of his back and focused his attention on Laila.

Laila held her own against Maurice. She gave just as well as she got. Maurice slammed Laila on the floor. When she hit the floor, her head hit the corner of the dresser. Laila lay there motionless. Cymone crawled to her mom and shook her. She rolled Laila over and noticed blood coming from her head. She jumped up and started swinging on Maurice.

"You bastard. Look what you've done."

Maurice didn't try to block Cymone punches. He just stood there and let her hit him. When Cymone stopped swinging he grabbed her by her neck and threw her on the bed. He ripped her shorts and panties off.

Cymone screamed. "NO... Maurice get off me!"

He unzipped his pants and freed himself. He grabbed Cymone's arms and pinned them to the bed. He parted her legs with his knees and forcefully entered her. Cymone screamed and bucked against Maurice, trying to get him off of her. He punched her in the face and told her to be still. Cymone stopped moving, but the tears flowed like a faucet. Maurice didn't care that she was crying. It seemed to excite him more. When he was finished, he looked at Cymone with a big smile on his face. "Was it as good for you as it was for me?"

Cymone just lay there crying. Laila was still on the floor unconscious, so they thought. They had no idea Laila was dead. Cymone got up and put her shorts back on. She noticed her mom was still lying on the floor, and she hadn't moved. Cymone walked over to Laila and sat down on the floor beside her. She placed Laila's head in her lap and stroked her face softly. "Ma, wake up." Cymone stared at Laila's chest to see if she was breathing. When she didn't see her chest rise and fall, she placed two fingers on her neck to see if she could feel a pulse. Cymone started frantically shaking Laila. "Ma, wake up. Wake up, ma."

Laila would never open her eyes again. Cymone screamed and hollered. Her mom was gone because of her mistakes. When she looked up at Maurice, he had a big smile on his face, and that pissed her off. She saw the gun on the nightstand beside the bed. She laid Laila's head on the floor and stood up. By the time Maurice realized what she was doing it was too late. Cymone had the gun pointed at him.

Maurice held his hands up. "Mone put the gun down?"

Cymone spoke her next words with no emotions. "Your sole purpose on this earth is to make my life miserable. You have taken everything I love away from me. Today was supposed to have been the happiest day of my mom's life. She was getting married to the only man she has ever loved." Cymone raised the gun to her head. "Are you happy now?" She closed her eyes and pulled the trigger. The gun clicked, but nothing happened. Cymone opened her eyes just in time to see Maurice lunge at her.

Chapter 23

Everybody had gathered at the church, but there still was no Cymone or Laila. The wedding was to begin in fifteen minutes and Steve was starting to get nervous. Steve walked over to Christi. "Hey Christi. Have you talked to Mone?"

"No Mr. Steve, I haven't. I've been calling her cell phone but she's not answering. We stopped by her apartment on the way here and she wasn't home."

"No, she stayed with Laila last night. They had mother/daughter time and sent me to sleep in a motel."

Christi smiled. "I guess that's why she didn't call last night. Have you tried Ms. Laila's cell?"

"Yeah, and the house phone," Steve responded. "I'll give them ten more minutes."

Christi could see the worry in Steve eyes. "Mr. Steve, Ms. Laila really loves you. All she has talked about for months was this day. Trust me she wouldn't miss it for the world."

Steve smiled nervously. "Thanks, I really needed to hear that because I was starting to think she had a change of heart."

Forty-five minutes passed, and Cymone and Laila were still a no show. Steve couldn't take it anymore. He had been calling, and there still was no answer. He knew something had to be wrong because they would have returned his call by now. Steve walked to the front of the church. "May I have your attention, please? I want to thank each of you for coming out today to share this moment with Laila and myself. I'm not sure why she hasn't gotten here yet, but I'm starting to get worried. I've called my daughter's phone and she's not answering. I've called my future wife's phone and she's not answering, and that's not like either of them. I'll understand if you all would like to leave, but I have to go check and make sure my wife and daughter are okay." Steve headed to the door, and Christi and Tasha were right behind him.

They pulled up to the house and saw Laila and Cymone's car parked in the driveway. Steve opened the door and yelled. "Laila, Mone... Are you here?" He walked through the house calling their name, and he still didn't get an answer. When he walked into the living room he noticed the broken lamp on the floor. He ran to the bedroom but found nothing. He opened Cymone's bedroom door and what he saw knocked the air out of him. "NO...." He stumbled back, in shock.

Christi and Tasha were right behind him. "What's wrong Mr. Steve?" Christi asked.

When Christi looked inside Cymone bedroom, she screamed. She ran inside and kneeled down beside Mone. She called her name and shook her. "Mone. Mone. Wake up Mone."

Tasha went into the room to check on Laila. She noticed the pool of blood under her head. She checked for a pulse and didn't find one. Steve stood there frozen. He couldn't speak. He couldn't move. Tasha pulled out her phone and dialed 911. She gave the 911 operator the information and the operator assured her help was on the way.

The paramedics arrived and pronounced Laila DOA. The paramedic checked Cymone. "She has a pulse." He started prepping her to be moved. They loaded Cymone on the stretcher and hurried her out.

Steve still could not move. He couldn't believe what had just happened. What was supposed to be the happiest day of his life turned out to be his worst nightmare. "Who would do this to my girls? Who would do this, on this day?"

"Mr. Steve I am so sorry for your loss. If you want to go to the hospital Christi and I will drive you." Tasha said, with tears in her eyes.

Steve just nodded and followed behind the girls. The ten-minute ride to the hospital seemed to take forever. When they finally arrived at the hospital, Christi walked up to the nurse's desk. "We're here for Cymone Jones. She was brought in by ambulance."

The nurse looked down at her folder. "Who are you to the patient?"

"I'm her best friend." She pointed at Steve. "That's her father over there. He's a little out of it, so I'm here to help him out."

"Ms. Jones is in surgery. The doctor will be out shortly to answer any questions you may have." The nurse kindly pointed to the waiting area for her to have a seat.

Christi thanked the nurse and walked over and sat between Tasha and Steve. She was hurting. Not knowing if her best friend was gonna make it was an emotional turmoil she had felt once before, and this time seemed much more real. But instead of breaking down she had to be strong for Steve and Tasha. She couldn't imagine the pain he must be feeling. He lost his fiancé on their wedding day which just so happen to also be the day he lost his only son. His daughter was in surgery, once again fighting for her life. Christi couldn't help but think Maurice was responsible in some way.

Two hours passed and the doctor finally came out to talk with them. "Ms. Jones has been viciously beaten and raped. She has blunt force trauma to her head and a broken back. It's too early to determine the damage to her spinal cord. Once the swelling goes down we will check to see if she has any feeling in her lower limbs, but until then we just have to wait and pray for the best." The doctor relayed.

"Can we go in to see her?" Christi asked.

"Yes, you can go in to see her."

Christi, Tasha, and Steve walked in Cymone's room, not knowing what to expect with the information they had just received. Cymone was resting comfortably. There were tubes running everywhere, and machines beeping consistently. The sight was too much for Christi to bear. With tears in her eyes, she turned and ran back out of the room.

Tasha looked at Steve with apologetic eyes and offered up a brisk apology. "I'm gonna go check on her."

Steve acknowledged her with a slow nod of his head. Standing there, looking at his baby girl, he was overrun by a swarm of emotions. He knew his father

[280]

wouldn't approve of him crying, but how could he not cry. His father's words played in his head. "Real men don't cry, a man who cries is weak, no son of mine is weak, dry those eyes." He heard his father's words as if he were standing right beside him. He knew at that moment he was a big disappointment to his father, but how could he be strong when the love of his life was gone, and his only baby girl was fighting for her life?

Steve sat down in the chair beside the bed and grasped Cymone's hands in his own. He closed his eyes and sent up a silent prayer to God. He knew without a doubt, God could heal Cymone. If anything could, it was him. All he had to do was have faith as tiny as a mustard seed.

Dr. Wright walked into the room. Steve wiped his eyes and stood up. Dr. Wright waved his hands. "No, no, no don't get up, stay there with your daughter. I just wanted to come in and check on her."

Steve returned to his chair. "Doc, when is she gonna wake up?"

"Mr. Jones, honestly, it's a waiting process. The morphine drip will have her out of it for a few days. She may wake up today, tomorrow, or next week. The rest will help with the healing process. Don't worry, she's in good hands. We will provide her with the best care possible. "

Without looking up Steve replied, "Thank you."

The next few days were hard for Steve. Trying to be at the hospital with Cymone while also trying to make funeral arrangements were taking a toll on him both mentally and physically. He wanted to hold off on finalizing the funeral, but after the ninth day he decided it was time to lay Laila to rest. He knew Cymone would be upset, but he couldn't put off the inevitable any longer.

****

The day after Laila was laid to rest, Cymone woke up. Steve wanted so bad to be by her side when she opened those beautiful gray eyes, but he wasn't there. As soon as he received the call from the nurse saying Cymone was awake, he grabbed his keys and headed to the hospital. The ten-minute drive it normally took to get there turned into thirty. Every car that was in front of him seemed to be going five mph. He finally made it and was surprised to see Tasha and Christi there also. Before Steve could ask how they knew Cymone was awake, Christi smiled before speaking.

"The nurse called me and told me she was awake."

Christi, Steve, and Tasha walked inside Mone's room and noticed she had her eyes closed. They thought she was asleep.

"She's asleep, let's just come back later and see her," Tasha stated.

Mone opened her eyes. "I'm not sleeping, I just have my eyes closed."

"How are you feeling baby girl?"

"I'm laid up in the hospital again, but this time it's not looking too good for me."

Christi rubbed Cymone's arm. "Don't worry and stress about things you have no control over. You still have your life, and that's enough to be thankful for. I'm here for you. Tasha is here, and so is Mr. Steve. We are all here to help you. All you need to do is focus on getting better." They visited with Cymone until the nurse announced over the intercom that visiting hours were over.

"Y'all can go and get some rest Mr. Steve, and Tasha. I'm gonna stay here with Mone tonight."

"Christi you don't have to stay here. Go home and get you some rest. I have a whole team of nurses to take care of me."

"Yeah, that may be true, but you also have a sister that's gonna be right here helping them, so get used to it. You're not getting rid of me that easily."

****

The day of the accident Maurice thought Cymone was dead, so he called Gina to come pick him up. When Gina picked him up, he made her promise not to say anything about what happened and if anybody asked her, he had been with her. Gina agreed to be his alibi.

They they arrived at Gina's place and instantly she started asking questions. She asked so many questions, she got on Maurice nerves. He kept telling her to shut up, but she didn't listen. Gina kept throwing question after question at him until he had finally had enough. He slapped Gina so hard she flipped over the sofa and hit the floor hard. She looked up at Maurice with tears in her eyes. Maurice smirked. "I told your dumb ass to shut up."

Gina didn't say anything. She just got up and walked to the bathroom. She got the rag off the towel rack, ran some cold water on it and washed her face. Maurice handprint was on her cheek, and her eye was bloodshot. When Gina walked back in the living room Maurice was still sitting on the sofa.

Maurice didn't look up when he heard Gina walk in the room. "Go fix me something to eat." He said in a condescending voice.

Gina didn't say anything. She just went into the kitchen and started preparing dinner. Gina wasn't a good cook, and Maurice let her know it when she put his plate in front of him.

Maurice scowled. "What the hell is this?"

"Rice and gravy, green beans and fried pork chops."

Maurice put a forkful of rice and gravy in his mouth and after chewing for a second, he spit it out.

Gina looked at him amused. "What's wrong, you don't like rice and gravy?"

Maurice looked at Gina like he wanted to kill her. "Yeah bitch, I like rice and gravy but I like my shit well done. This shit is crunchy as hell. Who taught you how to cook?"

"You should have gone in the kitchen and cooked for yourself," Gina said nonchalantly.

Maurice didn't say anything. He just got up and walked around the table. He stood over Gina and when she looked up, he punched her in the mouth. He politely walked back to his seat and ate the pork chops and green beans. Gina stood up and walked into her bedroom. When she came back out Maurice was sitting to the table acting like nothing had happened. He heard Gina enter the dining room, but he again refused to acknowledge her presence.

Gina held a gun to her side and spoke softly. "Maurice look at me." He pretended not to hear her. Gina said a little louder this time. "Maurice look at me."

Maurice let out an exasperated breath. He turned to look at Gina, but before he could say anything she shot him in the shoulder. The force of the bullet made him fall out of the chair. Gina walked over to him. She stood over him with the gun pointed in his face. She looked down with a smirk on her face. "Say something smart now Maurice."

Maurice looked up at Gina, with shock written all over his face. "Bitch, you better kill me. If you don't, you're as good as dead."

Gina laughed. "I don't think you are in a position to be making threats. I could have easily shot you from behind, but I wanted my bruised face to be the last thing you see before I send your worthless ass to hell."

Maurice laughed. "Bitch, you don't have the balls to kill me."

Gina shot him in the other shoulder. Maurice yelled out in pain. "Maurice I really loved you and I believed you when you said you loved me too. I was there for you when nobody else was. While you were whining about Cymone not being there for you, I was the one that kept money on your books. I was the one that was visiting you every weekend and accepting those calls from you every day. Who did you call to come pick you up? I could have easily said no and left you there to find your own way out of the shit, but no, my dumb ass got right up and came to pick you up. Do I get a thank you? No. I get slapped across the face and punched in the freaking mouth."

"Gina you need to calm down and put the gun away. I'm sorry for hitting you, but you have to understand I'm under a lot of pressure."

Gina looked deranged. "Oh, you sorry now. Just a few minutes ago I didn't have the balls to kill you. Maurice, the way I'm feeling right now, I'll blow your ass away and won't think nothing else of it. You don't want to go to jail for the rest of your life, so I'm not worried about you killing me. I got two words for you. SELF DEFENSE. When the police get here and see my face, and I tell them what you did to Cymone and her mom, do you honestly think they'll arrest me? You know what Maurice I could kill you right here right now, but I'm not. That would be too easy for you. I want you to spend the rest of your miserable life behind bars."

"Bitch, jail can't hold me."

"You got lucky with the aggravated assault charges, but add kidnapping, two counts of murder and another aggravated assault and tell me what you get. You get life with no possibility of parole." Gina picked up the phone and dialed 911. She gave the operator her information and explained what happened. When the paramedics and the police arrived, Maurice was lying on the floor with a bullet in each of his shoulders. The officer asked Gina if she needed to go to the hospital. She declined and told him she would be fine. She told the officers that she had picked Maurice up from Cymone's house, and when they got to her house he confessed to killing them.

"When I started asking questions he got mad and hit me. I bought a gun a few months ago, so I shot him to keep him from killing me."

The officer explained to her that where he's going she will never have to worry about him again. Maurice was taken to the hospital to check his wounds. The bullets went straight through so there was no need for surgery. He was patched up and sent directly to jail where he was charged with murder, attempted murder, kidnapping, and assault.

Chapter 24

A year had passed since that awful July day. Cymone had her life, but life was useless without the people she loved. Her ma was now in heaven with her brother. Instead of having one guardian Angel she now had two. What hurt Cymone the most was the fact she wasn't able to attend her mother's funeral. She never got the chance to say goodbye. Oh, how she longed to hear her mom's voice. Steve had stepped up while her mother was alive, but he hadn't seen Cymone or JJ since the accident. You would think the tragic accident would bring them closer together, but Steve reverted to the deadbeat dad she knew. Cymone felt like Steve blamed her for Laila's death and in a way she also blamed herself. She knew Maurice was bad news, but she wanted to believe he loved her enough to at least try to change.

Over the past year, Cymone could count on both hands and feet the number of times she prayed and asked God to take her. Cymone thought back to the day that changed her life. After she had realized her mom was gone, she wanted to die. She grabbed the gun, put it to her head and pulled the trigger, but nothing happened. Maurice tackled her trying to get the gun away from her.

Mone was so hurt by what Maurice had done to her mom; she went ballistic. Cymone swung her hand that held the gun and cracked Maurice in the face. The blow didn't faze him it only infuriated him. Maurice threw a series of powerful punches to Cymone's face, breaking her jaw in the process. Cymone tried to defend herself but she was no match for the rage Maurice had inside of him. Maurice picked Cymone up and slammed her on the floor. Her body hit the floor with a big thud, momentarily knocking her unconscious. Maurice was relentless in his actions, he showed no mercy for Cymone. As she lay on the floor motionless he stomped her body merciless. Maurice stomped Cymone and screamed obscenities to her for what seemed like hours. Cymone lay there in and out of consciousness unable to feel anything. She knew Maurice thought she was dead because she heard the panic in his voice when he called Gina to come pick him up. "Why isn't he calling for help?" Cymone thought to herself. "He's gonna just leave me here to die."

Christi's voice brought Cymone back to the present. "Hey girl, we're back."

JJ ran full speed and jumped in Cymone's arms. "Mommy, Mommy I missed you." He said, planting kisses all over her face.

This was the highlight of the day for Cymone. Her baby boy came home every day from school excited to see her. Cymone had her days where she felt worthless, but JJ had a way of making her feel accomplished. If she hadn't done anything right in her life, she knew giving birth to Joshua Hayes, Jr. was her biggest accomplishment.

"I missed you too." Cymone said hugging her son. "Did you have a good day at school?" She asked.

JJ eased up onto Cymone's lap and wrapped his arms around her neck. "This boy in my class named Dennis Johnson said some pretty bad things to me today." JJ looked up at his mother sadly.

Cymone was taken aback by this. She had no idea what a 5 year old could have possibly said to make her baby this sad.

"What did he say baby?" Cymone asked in a calm voice.

"He said you in a wheelchair because you was too stupid to leave the man that killed my daddy."

Cymone eyes widened in shock and horror. "Why would a 5 year old say such a thing?" She thought to herself. Cymone was so shocked by the words her son had spoken she couldn't respond. Christi could see the devastation written on Cymone's face so she stepped in.

"Come here JJ." She said motioning for JJ to have a seat next to her. JJ climbed down off his mommy's lap and sat on the sofa next to Christi.

"JJ kids often repeat what they hear adults saying not really understanding what they're saying. What that boy said about your mom was mean and not true. Your mom dated the man that had your dad killed, way before your dad died. That man was jealous your mom had moved on. He went to prison and harassed your mommy. She thought if she was nice to him he would leave her alone. Nobody knew he was getting out of prison, so when he showed up at your Nana Laila's house on her wedding day they were surprised. Maurice is a sick man and what he did that day proved how sick he was."

"That was the day mommy got hurt, and Nana Laila went to be with God."

"Yes baby." Christi responded choking back emotions. This wasn't the conversation she wanted to be having with her 5 year old godson, but it was time he knew the truth.

"Is he gonna get out of jail and try to hurt mommy again?"

Cymone finally found her voice. "Not if I can help it baby."

***

The day had finally arrived; it was time to face Maurice in court. Cymone, Tasha, Martha and Christi sat in the front row. Cymone wanted to speak to the court about what happened the day her mom died.

Judge McCarthy looked at Cymone. "Ms. Jones, are you prepared to give your statement to the court today?"

"Yes, your honor, I'm prepared." Cymone rolled her wheelchair and parked in the middle of the courtroom. She looked around at all the faces that were staring at her, ready to hear what she had to say. Cymone glanced at Maurice and froze. A vicious smirk snuck across his face as he stared her down. "Focus Cymone." Christi whispered loud enough for her to hear. Cymone looked at the her friends and family that sat on the front row for encouragement. She cleared her throat and began to relive that horrific day. "The day my mom and dad were to be married, Maurice decided he wanted to go on a rampage. He beat me and my mom. He raped me while my mom lay bleeding on the floor, and when I realized my mom was gone, I lost my will to live. I grabbed the gun to shoot myself; it clicked but nothing happened. Maurice tried to

[293]

take the gun from me. We fought and I ended up hitting him in the face with the gun. He picked me up and threw me on the floor where he began stomping me. I was in an out of consciousness so I'm not sure how long that lasted."

Cymone shifted in her wheelchair, as the people of the court watched, listening intently as she told her story. "I wanted so bad to believe Maurice could change. The entire time he was locked up he called me and wrote me letters confessing his undying love for me. While I was lying on the floor unable to move, not once did he try to call for help. He called Gina to come pick him up. Maurice literally left me there to die. When he told me about how he saved Nick from his stepfather when they were children, I felt that maybe he had changed, maybe he had a heart after all. My stupid self ended up forgiving him. Your honor, not only did I forgive him but I told him I would get back with him. I had found out that he had my boyfriend, the father of my son, killed. Yet I was still considering taking him back. I have to live with the decision I made at that moment to keep in contact with him, for the rest of my life. If I hadn't of invited Maurice back into my life, my mom would still be here, she and my dad would be married again, and I wouldn't be confined to this wheelchair." Cymone turned to Maurice, staring bleakly   in his eyes. "You have taken

[294]

so much from me. You knew my mom meant the world to me, but that didn't stop you from taking her away from me. Why did you even come to the house that day? That day was supposed to have been the best day ever. My mom and dad were getting married again. Do you know how long it had been since my dad was in my life? The day my mom died was the day my dad walked out of my life again. He blames me for her death, and I'm not mad at him for that because I blame me too. My son has to grow up without his father and his Nana all because of you. My son is five years old and kids are already saying cruel things to him. He doesn't deserve that. I hope you rot in prison for what you've done. You don't have to sit in prison wondering who I'm with now. Look at me. Who's gonna want me now? The one man that loved me, I mean truly loved me, you took him away from me. I pray you find peace within yourself. I pray you repent and ask God to forgive you. It hasn't been easy, but I prayed to God and asked him to remove the hate I have for you in my heart. It wasn't easy, but I've forgiven you. No need to smile because it's not for you. I had to forgive you in order to forgive myself. This is one less burden I have to carry around. I pray my mom can forgive me for allowing you back in my life. I pray that my dad can find forgiveness and return to my life." Cymone looked at Judge McCarthy. "That's all I have to say. Thank you for letting me speak."

Judge McCarthy addressed Cymone. "Ms. Jones, I can only imagine the pain and guilt you must be feeling. No one as young as you should ever have to endure so much pain. We all make mistakes. Your only mistake was you gave your love and trust to an unworthy man. Mr. Smith, please stand for sentencing. Mr. Smith, you pled guilty to the charge of murder, attempted murder, kidnapping, and aggravated assault. Is this correct?"

"Yes, your honor."

"I've been a judge for many years, and I've seen a lot of evil in my courtroom but never have I've seen evil like you. You have proven that you can't be a productive citizen. You have proven that you are indeed a danger to society, so with that being said Mr. Smith, I sentence you to life without the possibility of parole."

Martha got up and walked out after hearing the judge sentence Maurice to life without parole. She was hoping for the death penalty but knowing the bastard that was responsible for her son's death would spend eternity in prison gave her a sense of comfort.

Hearing life without parole made Maurice knees buckle to the point he passed out. Tasha and Christi looked at each other and burst out laughing.

"Damn, the big bad wolf ain't so bad after all. He heard life without parole and passed the hell out," Tasha blurted out.

Noticing Mone wasn't participating in their happiness, Christi asked. "Mone are you okay?"

Mone looked up with tears in her eyes. "I'm finally free of him, but look what it cost me. He has life in prison, but I'm also in prison. What quality of life do I have? I will never have any more children. I'll never walk or dance again."

"Cymone Jones. Stop with the pity party." Christi screamed. "I'm so sick and tired of you feeling sorry for yourself. Yes, you won't have any more but at least you have a son that loves you more than cupcakes. You probably will never walk again, so what you're still breathing. Your life is gonna be what you make of it. If you keep sitting here dwelling on the past, then you're gonna live a miserable life. The life you had is over and done with. You're gonna have to start living life in the present. God kept you here for a reason Mone. Maybe you can talk to young girls about your experience with Maurice. Show them what can happen if you don't get out. Don't let this stop you from being the beautiful, caring person that you are. Help somebody else with your testimony. I'm gonna be right here with you."

Cymone smiled. "I appreciate you Christi. You are gonna be a great mother one day. I know Christian would have been very proud to have you as his mother. Hell JJ is super proud to have you as god mommy and auntie"

"Thanks Mone that really means a lot."

"Okay, are y'all done with all this sentimental shit because y'all making me nauseous with this shit," Tasha huffed.

Christi and Mone both looked at Tasha. "Aww hush."

Chapter 25

When the girls arrived back to Christi's house, Tasha turned the TV on. She was flipping through the channels when something caught her eye. She turned the volume up when she saw a picture of Todd.

"The body found in a dumpster behind the Wal-Mart on Harrison Road has been identified as 30 year old Todd Walters from Charleston, South Carolina. If anybody has any information, please contact the Sheriff's department."

"Wow! I guess he fucked over the wrong female." Tasha said in disbelief.

"Are you okay Tash?" Christi asked.

"Girl yes. I came to terms with this a long time ago. I'm at peace knowing he won't be able to infect another woman," Tasha said.

"It's sad he went out like that," Cymone stated.

"Mone ain't nothing sad about how he went out. He got what he deserved. Todd was a danger to society," Tasha said. "That Nigga was good looking, intelligent and sweet. He could charm the panties off a nun if he was given the chance. I'm surprised you didn't sleep with his ass."

Mone smiled. "I almost did but something kept telling me to wait. He was always the perfect gentleman. He never tried to force me into anything. I ain't gone lie, I was really feeling him. We had great conversations. He took me bowling for the first time. One night I couldn't sleep, he called and ended up coming over. We sat in the backyard and talked all night long. When I found out he was HIV positive I knew right then it wasn't meant for me to be with anybody."

Tasha smiled. "He had you under his spell too. I give credit where credit is due. He knew how to treat a woman. The best sex I ever had was with him. Girl let me stop. You got me going down memory lane."

"There's nothing wrong with remembering happier times. Todd probably was a sweet person, he just didn't know how to cope with the fact that some chick had given him HIV," Christi threw in.

"That could be true Christi, but that still doesn't excuse the fact that he knowingly gave that shit to multiple people." Tasha looked out the window when she noticed a car pull up. "Are you guys expecting company?"

"I'm not. Mone are you?"

"No."

Christi went to the window to see who was outside. "Oh my God Mone, it's Mr. Steve." Christi opened the door before Steve could knock on the door.

"Hey is Mone here?"

"She sure is. Come on in."

When Steve walked into the house and saw Mone sitting in her wheelchair, a wave of guilt washed over him, and his eyes began to tear up.

"Mone, Tasha and I are gonna step out for a while to give you and Mr. Steve some privacy. I have my cell on me if you need me."

Once the girls were gone, Steve looked at his daughter and smiled. "Mone you look great."

"Thanks." She knew she looked like crap, but she welcomed the compliment even if it was a lie. "What brings you by here to see me after all this time?"

"Mone, I've been a jerk. I blamed you for something you had no control over and for that I'm sorry. All I could think about was my own pain. Being your father, I should have been there for you. Right now, I should be the one taking care of you and JJ, not your friend. It's just when I found out Maurice was responsible for Laila's death something in me snapped. We had been given a second chance at love and in a blink of an eye it was

[301]

taken away from me without warning. I don't blame you anymore Mone. I'm not saying I'm not disappointed in you for taking him back after everything he did to you because I am. You let a man in your life that wasn't worthy of you. Maybe that's my fault for not being there for you when you needed me the most. I should have been there to show you how a man is supposed to treat a woman. I should have been there to tell you how beautiful and worthy you are."

"Daddy, we can go on and on about the "what ifs" but it's not gonna change what happened. It hurt me so bad when you walked out on me again. When you walked out before it was okay because I had ma and Jarvis, but this time I had nobody. I'm stuck in this wheelchair for the rest of my life. If it was not for Christi and Tasha, I don't know where I would be right now. I couldn't have asked for better friends. I needed you daddy. I needed you more than anything in this world. I understand you were grieving, but so was I. You got a chance to say goodbye to ma. I wasn't given that opportunity. Not a day goes by that I don't think about her or the last night we spent together. I've been trying hard to forget the day Maurice took her away from me and put me in this wheelchair, but I can't. I sit here and pray I'm dreaming and I'm gonna wake up and everything will be normal again. Do you know how that feels daddy?

Do you know how it feels to live in a nightmare every single day? Do you know how it feels to want to go outside and run with my son and can't?"

Steve looked at Mone with so much compassion in his eyes that her eyes became watery. "Don't feel sorry for me daddy. I made a choice, and now I'm living with the choice I made. You made a choice to turn your back on me when I needed you the most, and that's what you have to live with. You're not here out of love. You're here out of guilt. I see the pity in your eyes, and I don't need nor want it."

"I am here out of love." Steve said unconvincing.

Cymone laughed. "Love would have brought you here a long time ago daddy. Guilt is what brought you here today. Ma has probably been haunting your dreams."

Steve didn't say anything, he just looked at his daughter because it was true. Laila had been coming to him every night telling him how disappointed she was in him. It had gotten so bad he was seeing her everywhere, not just in his dreams. He knew she wouldn't leave him alone until he tried to make things right with Cymone.

Cymone shook her head. "Just by the look on your face right now, I know I'm right. Ma comes to see me too. She talks to me all the time. She tells me to not give up on

[303]

life. To be thankful that I'm still breathing. This past year has been rough. Although I want to give up and throw the towel in at times. I know I can't because I have a little one that depends on me. What happened should have brought us closer together. We should have been grieving together."

"I realize that now baby girl. I want to be here for you, but if you don't want me here I understand. I just hope you will accept my apology."

"Daddy there's no need for apologies. I don't have any ill feelings towards you. I just don't have the room in my life for you right now. When you came back in the picture, I asked you to be consistent in my life. I love you daddy. I've always loved you, but my heart can't take you walking out on me again. You're gonna have to find a way to deal with the guilt ma has you feeling."

Steve stood up. "Mone, I'm really sorry for not being here for you, and I hope one day we can get back on the same page." Steve kissed his daughter on the forehead before he walked out of the door. Once outside the tears streamed down his face freely. He didn't know what to expect when he walked in to see Mone, but her turning her back on him was not what he was expecting. He had nobody to blame but himself. He could have easily reached out to her before now, but he let his stubbornness get in the way. When Steve reached his car, Tasha and Christi walked up.

"You leaving already Mr. Steve?"

Steve smiled. "Yes, Mone doesn't need me. I want to thank you for taking such good care of my baby girl. If you need anything don't hesitate to call me."

"Mr. Steve you don't have to thank me, Mone is my girl. Regardless of what we may have gone through in the past I love her and I will always be here for her and JJ."

Steve didn't say anything else. He just got in his car and drove away. Tasha and Christi walked in the house and noticed Mone looked happier than she did before they left.

"Why you look so happy?" Tasha asked.

"I feel like a weight has been lifted off my shoulders. The burdens I've carried around this past year are no longer with me. My dad came here to make amends with me, not because he wanted to, but because my ma has been riding him. I told him I didn't need or want his pity."

"Mone that's your Dad. He came here to make things right with you. Why wouldn't you let him?" Christi said.

"If he had of came a few months after my ma passed I would have accepted and welcomed him with open arms. I knew he was grieving because he and my ma had

[305]

just gotten back together, but he shut me out of his life completely. He didn't care how I was doing. He didn't check to make sure I was okay. For all he knew, I could have been stuck in some nursing home with people beating on me every day. Don't get me wrong I love my dad, but it's time I start loving me more. I've been sitting here for a year feeling sorry for my situation. I think it's time I start embracing it. Tasha I look at you and I say to myself, this girl is living with HIV, and she seems happier now than I've ever seen her. You haven't let the fact that you have HIV stop you from living, and I admire you for that. I'm stuck in this wheelchair for the rest of my life, and there's nothing I can do about that. So maybe I can try to keep it from happening to someone else."

Christi couldn't contain her excitement. "Does this mean what I think it means?"

"Yes Chris, I'm ready to share my story. I want to be a blessing to somebody like you have been a blessing to me. Maurice is in prison for life. I don't ever have to worry about him getting out, but I know it's only a matter of time before he tries to contact me. I stood strong in the courtroom and told him exactly how I felt. I don't know if I can stand strong with him calling confessing his love and saying he's sorry all the time."

Tasha patted Cymone on her knee. "Girl you can do it. You showed him in the courtroom that he didn't break you. I truly believe he won't be trying to contact you."

Christi tuned Tasha and Mone out. She needed to find out what prison Maurice was in and have him dealt with. Mone was finally accepting her situation and wanted to move forward, and she refused to let Maurice keep her down.

Epilogue

Maurice paced back and forth in his cell. He had only been in prison for two months, and it was already getting to him. He confessed everything because he thought Cymone was dead. When he saw her in the courtroom, his heart broke. Maurice did not know what it was about Cymone that made him so crazy. Maurice decided he would go out in the day room and play cards to get his mind off of Cymone and all the other bullshit he did. When he was out on the streets, Josh nor Nick had crossed his mind, not even that bitch of a mother, Laila had crossed his mind. Since he had been in prison, they were constantly haunting his thoughts. It had gotten so bad sometimes he thought he saw Nick working in the kitchen.

Maurice walked in the day room, "I got next."

Big Sam motioned for him to sit down. "You can come on and sit down, these dudes are up," he said. Maurice and the dude named Shine sat at the table. Maurice frowned when he found out Shine would be his partner. Everybody knew Shine did not know how to play spades, but since he was Big Sam's homie, they just played with him and took their loss like men.

"What's your name homie?" Big Sam asked.

"I'm Maurice," he replied.

"What you in here for Maurice?" Big Sam questioned.

"A little of this, a little of that," replied Maurice.

"I heard you killed four people," Shine added sorting his cards.

"Well, don't go around believing everything you hear," Maurice stated.

"So you didn't kill four people?" Shine asked again looking up over his cards.

Maurice gave Shine a dirty look. "Look, are we playing spades or ask a million questions?"

"My bad homie, I was just asking."

Big Sam pointed around the dorm. "In this dorm there are only murderers and rapist, which one are you? Are you a murderer like myself or a rapist like Shine?" Big Shawn probed.

Maurice looked at Shine. "Nigga, you in here for raping a bitch?"

Big Sam laughed. "Nawl, that nigga in here for raping multiple bitches."

"Damn…Well nawl, I ain't no rapist," Maurice said.

Before they could get the game started good the CO came into the room. "Sam you have a visitor."

Big Sam got up, and the guard escorted him to the visitation room. When he sat down, he could not believe who was sitting on the other side of the glass. He picked the phone up smiling. "This is a surprise...What the hell are you doing here?" He asked.

The visitor smiled back. "I wanted to talk to you about something," she responded.

"You couldn't drop a nigga a letter? I told you I didn't want you in this place." Big Sam scolded.

"Aww hush. You know you happy to see me." The visitor joked.

"You know I am, it's been like six years since I've seen you, you look good," Big Sam spoke. "How is everybody doing?" He asked.

"Everybody good," Christi said.

"What about your home girl Cymone, how she doing?" He asked.

Christi's eyes saddened. "That's what I wanted to talk to you about. I just don't know what to do." Christi stated. "See, she got involved with this dude, and he pretty much turned her life upside down." She explained.

Big Sam got comfortable in his chair. "I don't have nothing but time, so tell me about it."

"Well, he beat her so bad one time she was in a coma. When she finally left him, she got back with her ex-Josh." Christi said wiping the tears from her eyes. "Dude was so mad and jealous he had Josh killed while he was in jail. After Josh died Mone found out she was pregnant. Dude beat her mom up causing her death, and literally almost stomped Mone to death. He broke her back and now she's paralyzed.

"Damn…A lot has happened since the last time we talked. So, how is Mone handling all of this?" Big Sam asked.

"Sam, she blames herself for everything," Christi said throwing her hands up in defeat.

"You said he had Josh killed? Yo, you talking about nerdy Josh that Mone went with in high school?" Big Sam asked with a shocked look on his face.

"That's the one, but he wasn't that same nerdy kid he once was. JJ is the spitting image of Josh the only difference is he got swag at an early age." she said chuckling.

"Where is dude now?" Big Sam asked.

"I found out yesterday that he is in here with you," Christi responded.

"What's dude's name?" He asked.

"Maurice."

"Damn...I was just playing cards with a nigga named Maurice," Big Sam said with a puzzled look. "What dat nigga look like?" He asked Christi.

"He's about 5'10, maybe 150lbs, brown skinned with a scar under his right eye," Christi answered.

"Damn, I was playing cards with that Kat. My homie Shine mentioned dude had killed four people, but he denied that shit." He replied. "You want me to handle it? I know you and Mone are like sisters? Just give me the word," he said giving Christi a serious look.

"Sam...He raped me." Christi said with sadness in her eyes.

Big Sam's eyes got big. "Dat nigga what?" He boomed.

"He raped me and got me pregnant. I lost the baby though. He told Mone I took advantage of him while he was drunk, and she believed him at first," Christi said covering her face with her hand.

The anger Big Sam had was written all over his face. "What?"

"I had a miscarriage Sam. It was a boy, Christian Alexander Parker. He was so beautiful," Christi said allowing the tears to fall.

Big Sam looked shocked. "You named him after pops?" He asked. "Don't worry Lil' sis your big brother gone handle this. This nigga gone be taught a lesson," Big Sam said with a look of revenge on his face. "After tonight you won't have to worry about him again," he promised his sister.

The CO walked over to Big Sam. "Time up Sam." He said pointing at his watch.

"I love you Sis. Take care and whatever you do, don't come back here again." He commanded. "Send me a letter or something, but don't come back here. This is no place for you," he said.

"I love you Samuel." Christi said placing her hand on the glass.

Big Sam frowned. "Don't be calling me that in here." He grunted. Christi smiled and blew him a kiss. When she walked out of the prison, she felt relieved. Big Sam would take care of that situation for her. They were only six months apart, they shared the same father. Their mothers did not get along, so they never allowed them to have a relationship. Big Sam and Christi would sneak and talk to each other. They would meet up at games just to spend time together. Everybody thought they were a couple. Not too many of their friends knew they were actually brother and sister. Big Sam got locked up and given a life sentence for killing his baby mama and the dude she was with. Christi told him she would be there for him. She had started visiting him once a month, but Big Sam told her not to come back anymore because he did not want her to see him caged up like some animal.

When Big Sam got back to the day room, Maurice and Shine were still playing cards. Shine looked up and saw Big Sam. "Damn nigga…Who came to see you?"

"Nobody you know," he replied. "Maurice you play basketball?" He asked.

"Nawl, I'm no good in basketball, football my sport," Maurice responded looking over his hand.

"Cool, how about we get a game started when we go out in the yard?" Big Sam asked.

"That's cool with me. I need to work off some of this tension," Maurice said.

After playing football for an hour, Maurice took a shower. He enjoyed the hot water running over his body. Once he was done, he wrapped his towel around his waist and headed out. Before he could make it out the bathroom, he saw the guys he had played football with. He smiled. "The water still hot."

When he tried to pass by them, one of the guys jumped in front of him. "You leaving so soon?" He said.

"I'm done in here."

When Maurice tried to walk past again, one of the guys punched him in the face. Maurice looked stunned but before he could react, they all rushed him. They threw him down on the floor and kicked him repeatedly. A short stalky guy snickered. "I heard you like raping women."

Maurice panicked when he realized what was about to happen. He tried his best to fight them off, but it was six to one. They all took turns raping Maurice. After they were finished, he lay on the bathroom floor bleeding profusely barely able to move. Big Sam walked into the bathroom and saw Maurice lying there naked in a pool of blood. Feeling the presence of somebody Maurice looked up. "Help, he said reaching for Big Sam.

"Damn nigga, what happened to you?" Big Sam asked, faking concern. "You want me to go get the guards for you?" Big Sam facial expression became cold and menacing. "Maybe I should just leave you here and let you die." He growled. Maurice looked confused. "Let me ask you something. Do you know a girl name Christi?" Big

Sam questioned. Maurice nodded his response. "Well, Christi is my sister, she came to visit me today and she told me about a dude named Maurice. Do you know how surprised I was to find out she was talking about yo bitch ass?" Big Sam said kicking Maurice in the stomach. "My sister told me how you raped her, put her girl Cymone in a wheelchair, killed Ms. Laila and Josh." Wagging his finger at Maurice. "You have been a very naughty boy, but you fucked up when you touched my sister." Big Sam barked.

Maurice just closed his eyes and waited for the inevitable to happen. He had done so much dirt in his life. He knew one day karma would catch up with him. He just never thought he would go out like this. Big Sam pulled his shank from his pocket and sliced Maurice's neck from ear to ear. He stood over Maurice and glared down at his lifeless body. "You messed with the wrong nigga's sister."

KEEP IN CONTACT

FOLLOW ME ON TWITTER @AUTHORNICOLEH

INSTAGRAM @ AUTHOR_NICOLEH75

SNAPCHAT @ NICOLEYHILL75

FACEBOOK @ NICOLE Y HILL

OR EMAIL ME @ NICOLEYHILL75@ICLOUD.COM

CPSIA information can be obtained
at www.ICGtesting.com
Printed in the USA
LVHW012231050419
613134LV00015BA/312/P